Praise for
PERFECT FEAR

"*Perfect Fear* conveys a perfect, subtle terror: eerie, engrossing, almost Jungian, as it teases the subconscious. Richard Poe evokes Edgar Allan Poe, H.P. Lovecraft, Algernon Blackwood and other masters of horror."

—ROGER CORMAN, Academy Award-Winning Producer/Director
The Masque of the Red Death, The Pit and the Pendulum, Little Shop of Horrors

"As a filmmaker, it's really exciting to read stories that are cinematic in scope and style. I loved *Perfect Fear*. Richard Poe has tapped into real primal fears that we all experience—including some of my own childhood fears!"

—PAUL BALES, Chief Operating Officer, The Asylum
Producer, *Sharknado, Sharknado 2, Mega Shark vs Giant Octopus*

"The stories in *Perfect Fear* are riveting and really kept me on edge. Bravo to Richard Poe. Very good stuff."   **—CONSTANTINE MAKRIS, Director**
Orange is the New Black, Warehouse 13, Law and Order

"Moves with cinematographic speed . . . abundant outpourings of blood . . . bitterly funny . . ."   **—NINA ZIVANCEVIC, author of**
Death of New York City, Inside & Out of Byzantium, Living on Air

". . . intelligent and creepy . . ."

—PAUL GERMANO, author of "Lunch Hour" and other horror stories

"Classic horror . . . in the spirit of the Gothic masters . . ."

—DAVID YEAGLEY, author of *The End of the World in Poe*

PERFECT FEAR

FOUR TALES OF TERROR

RICHARD POE

HERAKLID BOOKS
NEW YORK CITY

HERAKLID
BOOKS
A Division of Heraklid Inc.

Perfect Fear: PUBLISHED BY HERAKLID BOOKS
a division of Heraklid Inc.

Cover design by David Ter-Avanesyan and Vanessa Perez
Interior design by Vanessa Perez
Cover images: Empire State Building by Philippe Bara; Chrysler Building
 © Clker.com; portions of city skyline © psdGraphics
Author photo by James J. Kriegsmann Jr.

Printed in the United States of America

First Edition, Third Printing, Third State

12 11 10 9 8 7 6 5 4 3
First Printing, July 5, 2012

Library of Congress Control Number: 2012941937

ISBN-13: 978-0615654713
ISBN-10: 0615654711

To my wife Marie, whose love sustained me and whose wisdom guided me through every step of this journey. *Perfect Fear* is her book, as much as mine.

He who sets out to fight monsters should beware lest he himself becomes a monster. Whoever looks into the abyss, the abyss looks also into him.

Friedrich Nietzsche
Beyond Good and Evil, 1886

CONTENTS

SCOTOPHOBIA

SCOTOPHOBIA

The scream cut through his slumber like a steel scythe. His wife was screaming. Even in his sleep, fear pierced him through and through. *It's happening,* thought Frank Romain. *The worst has finally happened.*

Every New Yorker has his own idea of what the "worst" might be. It might be an armed intruder standing on your fire escape, silhouetted against your window. It might be the tinkle of broken glass, the groan of a burglar's crowbar, or the crash of a sledgehammer against your steel window grate. These are the sorts of things most men would fear if they heard their wives screaming in the dead of night. But Frank Romain was not like most men. Burglars and murderers held little terror for him. He did not fear creatures of flesh and blood. The things Frank feared were invisible. Some might say imaginary.

Frank's therapist referred to his condition as scotophobia, a morbid fear of darkness. The word came from the Greek root *skotos,* meaning darkness, and *phobos,* meaning fear. When Frank first heard it, he conceded that scotophobia was probably as good a word as any. It was clean and simple, as medical terminology ought to be. But it was not exactly the right word. For, in truth, Frank did not fear the dark. Not the darkness itself. What he feared were certain things which he imagined might be lurking in the dark. And Frank was imagining those things tonight.

As Miranda's scream tore him from sleep, Frank's half-dreaming mind peopled the apartment with an array of ghastly beings. He imagined dead things ripe from the grave shuffling around his bed. He imagined them scraping their rotting fingers over Miranda's skin as she screamed. Yes, this was the worst, Frank decided. The very worst. And it was finally happening. Tonight.

"Uhhhh!" Miranda groaned, her voice filled with loathing and disgust.

"Miranda, what is it?" cried Frank.

He fumbled on the floor for his glasses. Miranda had leapt from the bed, shaking her leg as if it were on fire. "Get it off me! Get it off me!" she cried, grimacing in horror.

In the dim light that filtered in from the bathroom — a light which Frank always left on at night — Frank saw something tumble off Miranda's side of the bed. It was alive. The creature was shiny, reddish-brown, and about two inches long. It hit the wooden floor with an audible click and went scampering off into the shadows.

"Miranda, what's going on?" said Frank. He was fully awake now. His glasses had brought the room into sharp focus. The dream world was receding now, and the real world taking its place. Whatever was happening to Miranda, at least Frank knew that it was not *the worst*. Not tonight, anyway.

Slowly, through the dullness of sleep, Frank figured out what had happened. He recognized the reddish-brown thing scampering across the floor. If life in an East Village tenement had taught him anything, it had taught him to recognize the many varieties of vermin which shared man's urban habitat.

"It was a waterbug," said Miranda, still in shock. "I rolled on top of it. I could feel it squirming under my thigh. Ugh!"

Frank regarded the bug, which had now taken cover beside a pile of books on the floor. It hid in the shadow of one overhanging tome. New Yorkers called these creatures waterbugs, but they were actually giant cockroaches, of the species *Periplaneta Americana*. Urban legend often exaggerated their size to preposterous extremes, but this particular specimen was of normal dimensions, not quite two inches in length. A loose sneaker lay nearby. Frank shooed the bug from its hiding place and slapped it hard with the sneaker. He used a wet paper towel to clean up the mess. It was all very easy and matter-of-fact. But then, quite suddenly, it was over. The crisis had passed. There was nothing left to do. Silence fell like a stone. Deep shadows covered the room. "What now?" Frank asked himself.

The clock on the wall said 2:30 am. Frank groaned aloud. Just his luck! This was the worst time of night to be awake. Miranda would fall asleep quickly, but Frank would not. He would be alone in the dark through that long, desolate hour between three and four in the morning. And he would be afraid. All his life, Frank had a tendency to wake up around this time. It was a curse he could not seem to break. When he studied comparative folklore in graduate school, Frank learned that he was not the first to suffer from this particular curse. Many people through the ages had dreaded the hour between three and four in the morning. In parts of England, they called it the devil's hour. Further east, it was known by a different name.

The Russians called it *chas volka*. The Swedes called it *vargtimmen*. Both had the same meaning. It was the hour of the wolf, the time when wolves howl at your door. Every scotophobe knows the meaning of that hour. One of history's more prominent scotophobes, Swedish film director Ingmar Bergman, had explored the topic in his 1968 film, "The Hour of the Wolf." In it, Max von Sydow plays an artist descending into madness. He cannot sleep, for fear of the dark, so every night he keeps a nervous vigil through the wolf hour. He explains to his wife, played by Liv Ullman, that the wolf hour is the time when most people are born and most people die. "Now is when nightmares come to us," he tells her. "And if we are awake, we are afraid."

"Great," said Frank aloud. "That's just great. Here I am wide awake and the wolf hour starts in thirty minutes."

"Oh, please, Frank. Don't start that," said Miranda. "There's no such thing as the wolf hour. You really need to get a grip. You're not Max von Sydow and I'm not Liv Ullman. Please stop talking like that and come back to bed."

That was easy enough for Miranda to say. She did not suffer from scotophobia. She would have no trouble going back to sleep. But Frank knew that many hours of darkness lay ahead. He was quite sure he would sleep no more that night. "I'm going to the store," he announced to Miranda suddenly.

"But Frank, it's 2:30 in the morning. Why do you have to go out now?" Miranda pleaded.

"We have to kill the waterbugs," said Frank. "If there's one waterbug in here, there's probably more. We have to spray. I'm going to get one of those cans of heavy-duty roach spray."

Miranda frowned. "Okay," she finally said. "But be careful. It's dangerous out there."

II.

It was indeed dangerous, as Miranda said. The particular block of East 13th Street where Frank and Miranda lived was probably one of the more perilous districts of the East Village. Drug dealers filled the sidewalks, day and night. Things got violent sometimes. Now and then, gunfire broke out in the street. But, in Frank's view, these were minor inconveniences. Frank loved this neighborhood. It was the perfect place for a scotophobe.

The streets were always full of people, day and night. Of course, many of those people were drug dealers, crackheads and worse. But at least they were human. They could shoot you, stab you, rob you or beat you, but they couldn't do anything, well, *worse*. Frank loved walking out of his building at 2:30 in the morning, as he was doing tonight, and emerging onto a street that was aboil with activity. His block was a deep canyon of brick walls and fire escapes. On that hot summer night, shadowy figures in sleeveless t-shirts moved in the gloom. Dominican merengues blared tinnily from boomboxes. Vomit and urine steamed from the pavement. On the corner of Avenue A, the 24-hour Korean grocery store glowed like a beacon. "I love New York," thought Frank, with a deep sigh of contentment.

In New York, you were never alone. As long as there were crowds in the street, as long as there were neon-lit bars, fluorescent 24-hour minimarts, subways roaring underground and sirens ululating into the night, then all was normal. Everything was under control. It was different upstate. Frank was born and raised in a place called Donkerkerk, New York, a small town about a hundred miles north, in the Catskill Mountains. There, the half-dozen shops on Main Street closed early. Even the bars shut down at two in the morning, and once the last drunken drivers had vanished from Route 23C, a deadly silence hugged the forest.

Too many times, Frank had found himself driving alone down mountain roads under the awful ebon sky. Too many times, while his father slept off his latest drunk on the livingroom couch, Frank had lain awake in his bedroom, listening for that tell-tale sound in the woods, that broken twig, that growl from the dog, that odd new shrillness in the cricket's song that might signal *the worst* was on its way, lumbering across the yard on misshapen legs. Frank had never seen a ghost or a ghoul. In fact, he did not believe in such things, at least not in the daylight, when there were people around. But things seemed different in the dark. On wintry nights, when the moon gleamed and the naked trees scratched at his window, Frank knew that anything was possible. Anything.

When he was growing up in the Catskills, Frank liked to go with his friends to a place called Lookout Point. On a clear day, you could see four neighboring states, including Connecticut, Massachusetts, Vermont and New Hampshire. On certain nights, when conditions were right, you could see a halo of orange light gleaming on the southern horizon. That was the glow from New York City, a hundred miles away. Frank never tired of staring at it. Many times, he vowed to himself that he would live there someday, under that great dome of light. In the city, the lights never went out. Frank knew he would always be safe there. At least, so he imagined.

Eventually, Frank achieved his goal. He was accepted into New York University, and moved to Manhattan. There he earned an undergraduate degree in anthropology, and began work on his Ph.D.

in urban archaeology. Life was good in the city. In Manhattan, the tall buildings blocked out the sky, and the city hugged you close like a womb. The lights blazed twenty-four hours a day and the boundary between this world and that other world grew very thick. Frank liked it that way.

III.

Frank returned that night from the Korean minimart with a large blue and silver canister of Raid MAX. Though it was nearly 3 am, his tenement building still quivered with life. Beyond his apartment walls, above, below and all around him, hundreds of fellow tenants lived out their lives like bees in a great hive. Even now, at this hour, many would be eating, drinking, reveling, watching television or perhaps making love. Even now, Frank could hear water rushing through the pipes from his neighbors' showers, sinks and toilets. He could hear merengues wafting faintly from the sidewalk below, and jet planes thundering overhead, as they made their final approaches to Kennedy and LaGuardia airports. All was well on East 13th Street. Or at least so it seemed.

"Frank, why don't you come to bed?" said Miranda. "You can do the spraying tomorrow."

"It'll just take a minute," said Frank. The truth was, Frank was in no hurry to go to bed. Going back to bed meant turning out the lights again. It meant lying alone in the dark, unable to sleep, perhaps for hours. Spraying for cockroaches seemed a lot more appealing. And so Frank went into the kitchen and pulled the spray can from its plastic bag. "Raid MAX Roach and Ant Killer," said the label. "Contains Cylathrin. Kills Fast, Kills Long."

Frank looked up at the cupboards, suspended in a long row over the kitchen. He had seen many roaches creeping down from those cupboards. Perhaps the creatures were hiding on top. Yes, the top of the cupboards seemed like a good place to start. Frank shook the canister of Raid MAX. It felt cool in his hand, like polished gunmetal. Raising his arm aloft, Frank pressed the button and sprayed. A noxious, chemical smell pervaded the kitchen as the mist jetted upward and over the top of the cupboards. The clock on the wall said 2:45 am. Neither Frank nor Miranda were prepared for what happened next.

IV.

At first, Frank thought he was seeing things. He thought his eyes might be out of focus. But it was really happening. A veritable river of insect bodies came pouring over the top of the cupboard. There were small roaches, little more than half an inch in length. But there were also great big waterbugs, two inches long. Some of the waterbugs were larger than normal, Frank noted. Several three-inch specimens landed with sickening thumps on his kitchen counter. Then, a much louder thump drew Frank's attention to the stove. What on earth could that have been? He hardly dared look. When he did, Frank saw a great, shiny-winged *Periplaneta* lying flat on its back on the stove, its yellow legs kicking spasmodically, as thick as the legs of a frozen prawn, and surely as meaty. Frank's heart quivered at the sight of this prodigy, four inches long, if it was a millimeter. Never before had Frank seen a waterbug of that size.

Such monstrous arthropods existed only in tall tales traded with horrified laughter over cappuccino in Second Avenue coffeeshops. They were urban legends, nothing more. Yet the creature on Frank's stove was no legend. It was real. Gooseflesh prickled Frank's skin. A troubling premonition stirred in his mind. But he had no time to ponder it. Things were happening too quickly. Bug after giant bug plunged over the top of Frank's cupboard, writhing and kicking as they struck the counter. Some fell with a bounce on the metal sink. Others plopped into water-filled pots and pans, where they floated dead amid strands of broken spaghetti.

"Frank, what on earth is that sound?" said Miranda. From the livingroom, she could hear the bug bodies click as they fell.

"You really don't want to know," Frank replied.

It was all over in about five minutes. The bugs were dead. A poisonous mist filled the apartment. Miranda rose from her futon in the livingroom to see the damage. Together, she and Frank surveyed the corpse-strewn battlefield that had once been their kitchen. It would be a long time before Frank felt quite comfortable eating food from those pans again.

"I can't believe there were so many of them," Miranda said at last, her voice filled with wonder. "And so *big*."

"Well, they're dead now," said Frank. "Now we can sleep in peace."

Alas, Frank could not have been more mistaken.

V.

They cleaned up the roach bodies on the sink and counter. But now Frank had to climb on a chair to see what lay atop the cupboards.

"Be careful," said Miranda, as Frank clambered unsteadily onto the chair. His eyes burned from the roach spray. Frank blinked twice and beheld a veritable blanket of dead roaches, stacked half an inch deep atop the cupboard. With a paper towel, he began gingerly grabbing up handfuls of them, careful not to squeeze too hard, lest he hear or feel the grisly crunch of their exoskeletons. Frank was a little squeamish when it came to bugs, if truth be told.

"What do you see up there?" asked Miranda. "Are they all dead?"

"They're dead all right," said Frank, discharging his first load of roach bodies into the kitchen trash. "But I think our problems have just begun."

"What do you mean?"

"There's a big hole in the wall. I can just see the top of it from here, but I think there's more behind the cupboards. It's a huge hole. I think that's where the roaches are coming from."

"Oh my God," said Miranda. "Anything could come through there. There might be rats."

"It doesn't look like a rathole," said Frank. "It's more like the wall has rotted through."

"What are you doing?" said Miranda.

Still standing on the chair, Frank was leaning forward over the top of the cupboard, trying to get a closer look at the hole. But he leaned too heavily. The cabinet groaned beneath him. Suddenly, the whole row of cupboards ripped free from the wall. Frank barely had time to jump before the whole unit fell with a mighty crash over the counter and sink, shattering dishes and drinking glasses. The room filled with a fine gypsum mist from the broken wallboard.

"Frank!" Miranda screamed. "Are you all right?" She rushed to his side, grabbing his face in her hands and fussing over him. From below, the downstairs neighbors pounded angrily on their ceiling. "Cut out that friggin' racket!" called one muffled voice.

Frank sat on the kitchen floor, blinking in shock. His glasses had flown across the room. White dust clung to his face and hair.

"Yeah, I'm all right," he said, fumbling for his glasses. Frank regarded what had once been their kitchen wall. The cupboard, when it fell, had ripped out a gaping hole at least four feet wide. Through it, Frank could see the wooden wall studs within.

"Oh, look at our wall!" Miranda moaned. "It must have been completely rotted through. We've got to call the landlord. They have to fix this tomorrow. Frank, where are you going?"

Frank had disappeared into his office, at the far end of their railroad flat. He emerged, ready for action, with a flashlight in hand. His glasses were now secured to his head with a nylon strap. "I don't want my glasses falling off again," he explained.

The plaster dust was just beginning to settle. Frank's flashlight beam carved a weird corridor of phosphorescent mist through the air. Carefully, he and Miranda lowered the cupboard to the floor, exposing the hole completely.

"Nice, huh?" Frank remarked. "That hole must have been hidden behind that cabinet since we moved in here. No wonder this place is infested. Here, give me a hand."

With Miranda's help, Frank pulled the refrigerator away from the wall, exposing more of the hole. It was much larger than they had thought. Frank poked his head through and looked inside. For a long time, he peered into the depths of his kitchen wall, darting the flashlight beam here and there, his brow wrinkled in puzzlement. "Now that's the damnedest thing," he finally said.

"What do you see?" asked Miranda.

Frank withdrew from the hole. For a long time, he stood silently, biting his lip and tapping the flashlight thoughtfully against his palm.

"Frank, what is it? Will you talk to me? You're getting me scared."

"I don't see how it's possible," he finally said. "The wall just isn't thick enough. Unless, of course, it gets thicker on the floors below us."

"What are you talking about? Thick enough for what? What did you see in there?"

"Take a look yourself."

Miranda grabbed the flashlight and leaned into the hole. At first, she could not comprehend what confronted her. Just inside the hole, the wall appeared to be of normal thickness, about six inches wide. But when Miranda looked down, toward the floor, she saw that the space widened into a stairway, a red-brick, spiral staircase leading down into the gloom below. Miranda gulped and withdrew her head.

"There's a staircase in there," she said quietly.

"It looks to me like there's got to be a good six feet of clearance to make room for that staircase," said Frank. "The floors below us must have walls that are seven feet thick, at least."

"How can that be?" said Miranda.

Frank shrugged. "These are old buildings. Maybe they used to put service staircases in the walls to sort of, you know, get access to the plumbing. Or something." But even as he spoke, Frank knew he was talking nonsense. As a doctoral candidate in urban archaeology, Frank was intimately familiar with the architecture of nineteenth-century tenements on the Lower East Side. No stairways had ever been found in the walls of these buildings.

Clearly this was no ordinary staircase. It was a secret passage, built for some unknown purpose, more than a hundred years ago, by people long dead. Nothing in Frank's academic training had prepared him for such a discovery. He could not imagine what he might find at the bottom of those stairs. But he was determined to find out.

VI.

"I have to go down there and check it out," he told Miranda.

"You can't possibly be serious," she said. "How can you even think of going down that hole?"

Frank sighed. How could he explain his reasons to Miranda? He could, of course, pretend that his interest was purely professional. Frank was an archaeologist, after all. At least he *would* be an archaeologist, once he finished defending his doctoral dissertation next year. And this was a potentially significant find. After countless summers spent sifting damp earth in upstate New York for such meager rewards as broken arrowheads and tiny swaths of rotted Mohican basketry, here at last was something exciting — an actual secret passageway in the heart of Manhattan's East Village. A discovery like this could potentially find its way into a National Geographic television special. At the very least, it could get Frank a write-up in *Urban Archaeology Review.*

Frank had to admit, however, that professional ambition was not his driving motivation. His real reason was more primitive. It was the same reason that a child peers under the bed and checks the closet before retiring. Frank didn't like the idea of turning out the lights and going back to bed with that mysterious hole yawning in his kitchen. If he could just explore the passage a little, touch it, feel it, smell it, and see with his own eyes that no goblins crouched in its depths, Frank would feel a whole lot better about closing his eyes tonight.

"I should at least check the staircase to see if there are more bugs down there," Frank argued feebly, inventing excuses as he went. "If I don't spray now, they might come out of the hole while we're sleeping, and swarm all over the house."

Miranda shot him a skeptical look. "Okay," she finally said. "But wait for me to get dressed. If you're going down there, I'm coming with you."

VII.

They crept carefully down the dank, brick-lined stairwell, the last fading light from their kitchen receding above them. Frank led the way, brandishing his flashlight and the canister of Raid MAX. Now and then, he let loose a gust of spray when he spied a cockroach.

"You should save the spray," said Miranda. "Don't waste it on every little bug you see." *Because,* her mind finished silently, *you never know what we might find down below.*

The staircase seemed to spiral downward forever. The air was close and damp, the bricks mossy with age, and the staircase so narrow, their shoulders squeezed against the sides. After a very long time, Frank announced that he thought they had reached ground level. They had descended six floors. Frank tapped his flashlight against the bricks.

"This should be the Pinnellis' kitchen behind this wall," he said. "The basement is right below us."

He shined his flashlight down the stairwell, but it revealed only the same endless passageway, spiralling downward into infinity. Frank could discern no opening into the cellar. "Let's go," he said.

Soon they had descended to a point that must have been at least ten feet below the basement. But they had still found no opening. The staircase continued ever downward. Frank and Miranda stopped and looked at each other in the pale glow from the flashlight.

"I'm starting to get claustrophobic," Miranda admitted calmly.

"Me too," said Frank, with a nervous glance upward.

"If this staircase doesn't open out into something soon," Miranda suggested, "we go back up. Okay?"

"Fair enough," said Frank.

They resumed their descent. Both of their faces were now covered with a fine sheen of sweat. The air in the tiny passage had grown thick.

"Have you noticed something about the bricks?" Frank said.

"What about them?"

"They're different. Ever since we dropped below the basement. Above that level, they're the same bricks as the rest of the building. But now they're smaller and yellowish in color." With his finger, Frank wiped the dirt and grease from one brick. "Look here. Underneath all the crud, there's a sheen or glaze. These are 17th-century bricks. They have to date from the Dutch colonial period, no later than 1664." Frank's voice grew quiet with awe. "It's amazing," he said. "No one knows about this except us. It's a significant find."

"But Frank, why would the Dutch colonists build a spiral staircase going straight down into the ground?" asked Miranda.

"I guess we'll find that out at the bottom," Frank replied. They continued down the stairs.

"Uh, Frank," said Miranda, after a few minutes. "Isn't it about that time?"

"What time?"

"To start back up?"

Frank didn't seem to hear her. He was listening intently to something far below.

VIII.

"It sounds like water," said Frank. "Running water. Could be an underground stream. Or maybe a water main. It's not far."

Miranda sighed and followed. As they descended, the sound of rushing water grew closer. Suddenly, they reached the bottom of the staircase. The narrow stairwell opened out into a wide chamber. On this level, the 17th-century bricks gave way to an altogether different type of stone. Above and around them, Frank's flashlight revealed a great hall formed of limestone megaliths. The stones were gigantic, many as big as cars, and some even bigger.

"Frank, what is this?" asked Miranda, a small tremor in her voice.

Frank didn't answer at first. His mind had not yet processed what he was seeing. The huge size of these stones and the massive, post-and-lintel construction was unlike anything he had expected to find. Neither the Dutch colonists nor the Algonquin Indians had built anything like this. The great stone chamber reminded Frank of megalithic structures peculiar to certain prehistoric sites in Europe and South America.

Stonehenge came to mind, or Tiahuanaco in Bolivia. But this was not Bolivia. This was New York. These ruins were completely out of place here. They did not belong in Manhattan. *Can it be?* Frank mused silently. *A lost civilization? Right here in the East Village?*

"Frank, talk to me!" said Miranda. "What is this? Who built these things?"

"I have no idea," Frank replied. And indeed he did not. Conventional archaeology provided no clue as to who might have built such structures. Urban legend, however, offered a wealth of possibilities. New York's rumor mills had long dwelt upon the possibility of secret tunnels and ancient catacombs buried beneath the city. No one had ever seen these legendary stoneworks, yet rumors of their existence proliferated. Every occult bookstore, crystal therapy clinic and vegetarian juice bar in Manhattan abounded with theosophists, druidists, UFOlogists, psychedelicists and other New Age sectarians, eager to add their own peculiar embellishments to the yarn. Some attributed the mysterious stoneworks to Atlanteans; others credited space travelers from the Pleiades star cluster; seafaring Druids from ancient Ireland; or the lost fleet of the Knights Templar. Frank made it his business to collect such stories, as he collected all urban legends, no matter how odd or improbable. But this was no legend. This limestone chamber where he and Miranda now stood was real. Like the four-inch cockroaches lying dead in his kitchen, this megalithic chamber was an urban legend come to life. It was a thing that should not exist, yet existed nonetheless.

"Frank, do you think the Indians could have built this?" asked Miranda.

Frank frowned. "It doesn't seem likely," he mused. "The Algonquins erected cairns and standing stones for religious purposes, but, well, nothing like this. Look at the size of these stones. Some of these must weigh a hundred tons or more. Where did they quarry this limestone? And how did they transport the stones? This was a huge undertaking. There's nothing else like this in North America."

"Frank, shine your flashlight over here," cried Miranda. She pointed to one of the limestone blocks forming the wall of the chamber. The stone was slimy and dank. Beneath the grime, Frank saw pictographs. A figure of a large, coiled serpent wound its way across the megalith. Beneath the snake, Frank saw other symbols. They had the appearance of writing, but were unlike any script Frank had ever seen. The characters were jagged and keen, like shards of broken glass. They looked as if some madman had struck them from the rock in a fit of rage. It occurred to Frank that something was not quite right with these letters, but he couldn't put his finger on it. Disturbing images filled his mind. A wave of nausea unsettled Frank's stomach.

"Is that writing?" asked Miranda.

Frank swallowed hard and pushed the troubling thoughts away. "Yes, it does look like writing," he said. "But I've never seen this script. It's completely unknown." Frank pulled his mind back from the abyss. He reminded himself that he was a scientist. He must keep a level head. Few archaeologists ever got a break like this. It was important to stay focused. This was beyond anything Frank could have hoped to find when he started down that staircase. It was the find of a lifetime, a new civilization. This discovery would make him famous, Frank realized. The arteries in his neck throbbed in excitement. Frank rocked his flashlight back and forth across the giant stone archway before them. His flashlight revealed yet another chamber in the gloom beyond, a much larger chamber, by the look of it. "Let's check it out," said Frank.

He proceeded ahead, but Miranda hung back, afraid. "Frank, it's so dark in there. And we're getting too far from the staircase. Please, let's go back. This isn't safe. What if we get hurt or we can't find our way back? No one even knows we're down here. We should come back later, when we have help."

Frank wavered for a moment. On one level, he knew that Miranda was right. But it was too late to turn back now. Frank knew that the moment this find was reported, the tenured professors would move in, hogging all the glory and grant money for themselves. This was Frank's one chance to play the explorer, perhaps the only chance he'd ever get.

"Just a little farther," he told Miranda. "I just want to see what's beyond that doorway. We'll check it out, then we'll turn back. Okay?" Miranda nodded reluctantly and followed Frank through the massive archway into the blackness beyond.

IX.

The flashlight beam pierced the darkness. Wherever it shone, it caught a mist glistening in the air. The floor, Frank could see, was covered with puddles and slime. When he trained his flashlight on the ceiling, Frank saw long white stalactites which must have taken centuries to form. The sound of running water echoed through the chamber. It seemed to come from a long way off, from somewhere beyond the walls.

"Give me your hand," said Frank.

Cautiously, they stepped through the stagnant, limey puddles. Water seeped through their sneakers, oily and cold. The chamber was so immense that Frank could not find the other end of it with his flashlight. He saw only square limestone columns spaced at wide and regular intervals, stretching outward toward infinity.

"Frank, this floor isn't solid," Miranda said suddenly. Frank's flashlight beam darted downward. Too late, he saw that the ancient limestone was as pockmarked as an old Swiss cheese. Countless centuries of dripping water had eaten holes through it. Even the solid parts yielded like styrofoam beneath their feet.

"Miranda, I think we'd better go baaaa...."

Frank never finished his sentence. With a roar like thunder, the floor gave way beneath them. Flashlight and bug spray flew from Frank's hand. His glasses bounced wildly over his face, dangling from their nylon strap. For one mad second, only the rush of air past their faces and the sound of their own screaming told Frank and Miranda that they were still alive, as they tumbled headlong into the unfathomable gloom below.

X.

"Miranda, are you all right?" Frank cried desperately.

He had fallen into some sort of swamp or lagoon, choked with mossy fibers that clung to his skin. All around, he could hear the roar of rushing currents. It sounded as if there were rivers and waterfalls nearby, but he could not see them in the dark. Suddenly, he heard Miranda's terrified cry. *"I can't swim!"* she screamed.

"I'm coming. I'm coming," said Frank, plunging blindly in the direction of her cries. Soon, he felt her thrashing body in the darkness. He locked his arm clumsily around her neck, using a life-saving technique that he only vaguely remembered from some long-ago gym class.

Frank could just make out a shoreline of rough-hewn limestone blocks over to his left. He swam toward it. Moments later, he and Miranda lay on the stones, coughing, gasping and hugging each other, shivering with relief and terror. The darkness around them was black and deep. But a faint light glowed in the cavern. It shimmered over the water, rising and dissipating into the shadows above. What sort of light was it, Frank wondered? Where was it coming from? As his eyes slowly adjusted to the gloom, Frank peered into the ghostly glow, seeking its source. He did not have to look long. The light source was right in front of him. It was his own flashlight, which he had dropped in the fall. Now it was floating on the water, several yards from shore. Somehow, its watertight gaskets had held. Its bulb was still miraculously ablaze. With a shiver of fear, Frank realized that this flashlight was now their only hope, the only thing standing between them and total darkness.

"Honey, stay here," Frank said. "I've got to get the flashlight."

"Oh no, Frank. Please. Don't go. You don't know what's in that water."

"We've got to have the flashlight," he insisted. *Or we're lost*, his mind completed the sentence. But he didn't say that part out loud.

Lowering himself carefully into the cold water, Frank kicked away from the edge. He siezed the flashlight with a triumphant flourish. Mission accomplished! But, as he turned to make his way back to shore, Frank suddenly froze in the water, paralyzed by some primitive impulse emanating from deep in his limbic brain.

In the flashlight beam, Frank could see Miranda huddled miserably on the shore, tears pouring down her face, barely ten feet away. But something else had registered in his mind, just before. What was it? Frank swung the flashlight back in a wide arc. Yes, there it was again. A metallic reflection of some sort. Two red discs, hovering on the surface of the water, catching the flashlight beam like tiny bicycle reflectors.

At first, Frank's brain drew a blank. *A boat with reflectors?* he thought dumbly. And then, like a curtain parting in his mind, he remembered where he had seen this before. It was in a PBS documentary on television, a beautiful, haunting scene of the Florida Everglades at night, lit with dozens of pairs of tiny red disks, the reflective eyes of alligators lying low in the water, stalking their prey.

Alligators.

What followed next was a barrage of sensory input too overwhelming for Frank's conscious mind to absorb. He was hardly aware of the red eyes darting straight toward him, at terrifying speed. He barely noticed Miranda screaming on the shore, or the ache of his own muscles as he thrashed through the water, powered by a mighty surge of adrenalin. The only thing Frank really noticed was the flashlight, clenched in his hand. His iron grip never slackened for an instant. His nerves understood, even if his mind did not, that, if he lost that flashlight now, he would die in the everlasting darkness beneath New York City.

XI.

It seemed only a second before Frank was back at the shoreline, with the flashlight in hand. Miranda pulled frantically on his arms, as Frank heaved himself out of the water. Some inner calculation told Frank, however, that he had not swum fast enough. The monster was too close behind him. Frank winced in anticipation of the pain. At any moment, he expected the beast to close its jaws on his still-dangling legs.

Miranda screamed.

Frank heard behind him the sharp, wet slap of the alligator's jaws snapping shut. It had missed him! Frank scurried from the water's edge, the flashlight still clenched in his hand. The monster glared at him from the water. It was easily fourteen feet long. Converging on them from every direction, Frank saw at least a dozen more pairs of shiny red disks coursing through the murk, their lashing tails making oily reflections in the water. Frank's voice was so hoarse from screaming, it was hardly more than a whisper. "Miranda," he croaked. *"Run."*

Once more, PBS came to Frank's rescue. In that crucial split second, he remembered watching a National Geographic special about Nile crocodiles. He remembered how they stalked their prey. When they spied a wildebeest drinking at the riverbank, they would move in silently for the kill, gliding up close, then leaping right out of the water to grab their quarry from the shore. Frank learned from that special that crocodiles can jump. He later learned that alligators have that same ability.

"*Run!*" Frank cried.

The beast's terrible lunge nearly got them. They escaped by mere nanoseconds. The creature reared almost six feet from the water, snapping its jaws and landing on the shore with a loathsome, wet splat. Frank knew what was coming next. He knew that alligators could run up to twenty miles per hour on dry land, at least for short bursts, faster than any Olympic sprinter.

"Come on!" cried Frank, grabbing Miranda's hand. His flashlight wobbled crazily, illuminating a hellish tableau of red eyes, rough heads and scaly forelegs slapping out onto the stone shoreline. A brief sweep of the flashlight beam showed Frank the only way out, a thin, corbelled archway about five yards back from the water's edge. "Come on!" Frank cried again.

They slipped and slid through the opening, like baseball players skidding into home plate. An alligator plunged its muzzle through the archway, right behind them. The monster snapped its jaws, only inches from Miranda's kicking legs. She scrambled away on her back, kicking and screaming, her sneakers pounding against the alligator's jaws. In another moment, the creature would have her. But strangely, it did not pounce. It was stuck in the archway. Its scaly shoulders were too wide to fit through the opening. For one long, delirious moment, Frank and Miranda lay hypnotized, staring at those immense jaws snapping and straining like some demonic wind-up toy. Then they were on their feet and running for dear life.

XII.

Frank lost track of how long they'd been running. They emerged into a narrow corridor which split in two directions, to the left and right. They would have to choose which way to go. For a moment, they stood panting.

"Do you think they got through?" asked Miranda breathlessly. "The alligators?"

Frank shook his head. "I don't think so," he said.

Miranda sank heavily to the damp stone floor and shook her head. "How?" she said at last. "How could it be?"

Frank joined her on the floor. Both of them were soaked, and beginning to feel a chill. Frank put his arm around her.

"Pets," he said, his voice strangely distracted. "People buy baby alligators as pets. When they get too big, their owners flush them down the toilet. Some survive in the sewer system."

"I thought that was just a story," said Miranda, panting.

Frank nodded. Miranda was right. It was just a story. Technically speaking, it was an "urban folk belief." Frank had once written a paper about New York's alligator-in-the-sewer stories for Professor Russell Isherwood's urban folklore course.

"The legend of alligators supposedly living in the sewers of New York City," Professor Isherwood had lectured, "is one of the clearest examples we have of mythic formation in the modern city. It begins, as do all folk legends, with a rumor or proto-legend, in this case a series of sensational, but entirely groundless, press reports in the 1930s. Then begins the process of *communal re-creation*. Each time the story is passed from barstool to barstool, it grows a little in the telling. Each narrator adds his own embellishments, until finally we have a full-fledged urban folk belief, a tall tale which thousands, perhaps millions of people believe to be true, despite..." and here Professor Isherwood chuckled, "despite a complete lack of corroborating evidence."

But Professor Isherwood had been wrong. Those early newspaper reports had been far from "groundless." When Frank researched his paper, he found a plethora of well-documented accounts of alligators caught in the Bronx River dating back to 1932, and even one report of a seven-and-a-half foot specimen killed and retrieved from a Harlem sewer in 1935. A red-faced Professor Isherwood had given Frank a "C" for the paper. He added an angry marginal note urging Frank to be "a little less ingenuous, in future, in your assessment of primary sources."

Frank was more careful what he wrote after that. But the real lesson he learned was that the experts didn't know everything. Even the learned Dr. Isherwood had yet to discover that legends were not always fantasies.

"There's got to be a way out of here," Miranda was saying. "Frank, are you listening?"

Frank was not listening. His mind was following a train of thought that he did not want to follow. The idea of giant alligators living in the sewer was strange. But no one could deny that it was *possible,* at least in the physical, biological sense. Ditto, Frank thought, for the four-inch cockroaches that came leaping from the top of his cupboard. Ditto for the limestone megaliths buried beneath the streets of New York. Unlikely, yes. Impossible, no. All of these things could theoretically exist in the real world.

But something else couldn't, Frank realized. The staircase in the wall. What a fool he had been. Frank had seen the problem, but had chosen to ignore it. The spiral staircase was at least six feet wide. But the wall itself was only six inches thick. The staircase could not possibly fit inside the wall. Yet there it was, all the same. The staircase was unnatural. It violated physical laws. And that could only mean one thing. Reality had cracked tonight. Like the poor lost souls in Welsh legend who followed pixie lights into the bog, Frank and Miranda had strayed from the path. They had wandered like fools into the midnight realm of the other world. And, in that world — despite all the easy assurances of a thousand Professor Isherwoods in their classrooms — Frank knew that anything could happen. *Anything.*

"Do you... hear something?" Frank said at last, his voice feeble and hoarse.

"Just my heart beating," said Miranda.

"No. Stop and listen. There's something... down there." Frank gestured vaguely toward the blackness down the corridor to their left.

For what seemed a geological age, Frank and Miranda held perfectly still and listened. Only after their hearts quieted and their breathing had grown more regular could they begin to make out the sound. It was faint and far away, a rustling, dragging noise, like an army of wet scarecrows shuffling down a paved street. It was coming from the tunnel on the left. And it was coming toward them.

"What *is* that?" Miranda whispered, her eyes incandescent.

Frank tried to say something, but his voice would not come. His arms and legs shook like rags in the wind. His bladder felt painfully full. Frank forced himself to his feet and pulled Miranda up alongside him.

"We've got to go," Frank finally managed to squeak. "That way. Quick."

With a trembling arm, Frank indicated the only direction left open to them, down the tunnel to the right.

"What is it, Frank?" Miranda asked when they had jogged about 50 yards down the passage. "Is it the alligators?"

"No," Frank replied. "I think it's something worse."

XIII.

Even as he and Miranda hurried down the dark limestone passageway, Frank's mind drifted back to a dreary afternoon spent doodling in his notebook while Professor Isherwood expounded on the intricacies of Iroquois folklore. Frank remembered this as one of Isherwood's more tedious lectures. The professor's mind seemed to be wandering that afternoon. Perhaps the old man was getting senile, Frank had thought, at the time.

According to the class syllabus, Isherwood was supposed to be lecturing on urban folk beliefs in the New York metro area. Yet, for some reason, he had veered off topic, maundering on about some archaic superstitions of the Iroquois Indians. Frank knew that the Iroquois were a woodland people whose traditional lands lay west of the Hudson River, hundreds of miles upstate. As far as Frank knew, they had never set foot anywhere near the New York City area. So why was Isherwood talking about them? Frank scribbled furiously in his notebook, covering the page with whorls and curlicues, and digging deep, angry furrows with his ball-point pen.

Had Frank been listening more closely, he would have understood the reason for Professor Isherwood's digression that day. The professor had already explained that many Iroquois people had migrated down to the city from upstate New York, during the 1920s and '30's. Mostly they were Mohawks, looking for construction work. Mohawk ironworkers had built many of Manhattan's most famous bridges and skyscrapers. When they came to the city, they brought their folklore with them. Frank had missed that part of the lecture. He was too busy doodling. He filled many pages, that day, with squiggles, coils and geometric shapes. But, in the midst of his doodling, something caught Frank's attention. It was something Professor Isherwood had said. Something important. Frank stopped in mid-doodle and eyed the professor.

"The cannibal skeleton is perhaps the most frightening bogey of Iroquois legend," Isherwood was saying. "Technically speaking, it is a type of vampire or revenant, a dead person who returns to feed upon the living. The Iroquois people of upstate New York conceived of this creature as a skeleton, which would come to life by night and feast on human flesh. It goes by many names. The Mohawks called this creature *rahskahn*." Professor Isherwood pronounced the word somewhat differently than the way he wrote it on the chalkboard. He pronounced it LUS-kin.

Suddenly Frank was all ears. Instinctively, he sensed the importance of the professor's words. Frank forgot his doodling, leaned forward, and stared at Isherwood with piercing intensity. The *rahskahn* feared light, Isherwood told the class. It feared any kind of light, whether sunlight by day or campfires by night. Many Indian legends told of people pursued by the *rahskahn* who found refuge in some friendly village. In the light of the village fire, the monster could not touch them.

That was a good thing to know. But Professor Isherwood had said something else that afternoon. Frank was sure it was something important. But he could not remember what it was. As he raced down the dark passageway, beside Miranda, Frank strained to remember. He forced himself to think back on that long-ago afternoon, reconstructing every detail in his mind's eye. He visualized Dr. Isherwood standing before the class, in his trademark Scottish tweeds. Frank could see the professor's lips moving, just as they had moved that day. But what was he saying? Suddenly, Frank remembered.

"Don't look back," he gasped to Miranda.

"What?" she cried.

"Whatever you do," Frank panted, *"don't look back."*

XIV.

They had been jogging now for some time. Frank's glasses bounced over his face, held only by the loose nylon strap. Ahead of them, the flashlight beam played across the stones. The flashlight was running low on power. Its diminishing glow revealed only an endless, curving tunnel ahead.

All at once, the tunnel came to an end. It opened into a wide hall, whose ceiling had ruptured in some archaic cataclysm. Great lintels drooped from the roof like fallen giants. Tons of stone and rubble had poured in through the broken ceiling. A great pile of rubble blocked their way.

"We're stuck," said Miranda desperately. "It's a dead end."

Frank played his beam over the rubble heap. The stone pile rose all the way to the ceiling. At the top of the heap, he saw something promising. There was an opening in the ceiling. Pressure from the earth had pried two ceiling lintels apart, opening a gap between them. The gap was no bigger than a crawlspace. But a crawlspace was better than nothing. "We've got to climb," said Frank. "All the way to the top."

Without hesitation, Miranda scrambled up the rock pile. The stones were huge. Many had razor-sharp edges where they had fractured. The stones slashed and cut their skin as they climbed, leaving a bright trail of blood. Both had reached the limits of their strength. As they neared the summit of the rubble heap, Frank could hear once again those dragging, scratching sounds approaching from behind. They were closer now. Much closer. The damp breeze wafting in from the tunnel stank with a charnel-house reek. At the smell of it, Frank's strained bladder finally let go.

"Oh God, oh God, oh God," Frank babbled, his voice squeaking out several octaves higher than normal, as if he had inhaled helium.

"Frank, come *on!*" Miranda cried from above.

She had reached the top, and began squeezing up into the crawl space, through the gap in the ceiling lintels. Frank was right behind her.

"It's a passage, Frank. It goes further," Miranda called. She hoisted herself up through the ceiling, and crouched at the opening, waiting for Frank. He could see her beckoning, urging him on. He could almost touch her now. Yet, he was moving so slowly. Frank's muscles seemed like water. It took him forever to crawl over each jagged slab.

"Ahhhhhhhhhh!"

Frank's scream pierced the darkness. A shiver of pain lashed up his leg. He had twisted his ankle. Even worse, the flashlight had tumbled from his hand and lodged itself just out of reach between two immense stone slabs.

"Oh no!" cried Frank. "I dropped the flashlight. I can't believe it." As he groped frantically between the giant stones, Frank was only vaguely aware that he was crying, sobbing, babbling and moaning like a lunatic. "I can't believe it! I can't believe it!" he gasped in his high, helium voice.

"Oh Frank, hurry. Please hurry," Miranda was saying.

Then, all of a sudden, Miranda stopped talking. There were two or three long seconds of deathly silence, just long enough for Frank to start wondering what had happened to her.

When he looked up, he saw Miranda's face frozen, her eyes staring beyond him, wide as saucers, her lips quivering in fear. *She sees something,* Frank thought numbly. *She's looking at something right behind me.*

And then she screamed. In the diffuse corona of light filtering up from the fallen flashlight, Frank noted blankly and without emotion that Miranda had fallen to her knees, that her eyes bulged from her head as if they would fall out, that she screamed so hard, gobs of drool trailed from her mouth. She screamed again and again and again, until she ran out of breath. Then she raked in more air with a great, gasping wheeze and started screaming again.

Don't look back, said a quiet, urgent voice inside Frank's head. *Whatever you do, don't look back.*

It was all around him now, that fetid stench like a week-old carcass exploding with maggots. He could hear them too, not just the brittle clatter of their bony feet, but a whispering, breathing sound like the hiss of a snake, issuing from a hundred throatless mouths. Frank could hear the clitter clatter of their bony mandibles, as they worked their jaws and clicked their teeth.

Don't look back, said the gentle voice inside him.

"I won't, I won't," Frank squealed in his helium voice. Frank's ears told him his pursuers were at the bottom of the rock pile now. He could hear their hands and feet skittering on the stones like clothes pins. They were climbing up toward him.

"*Frank!*" Miranda screamed at last, finding her voice. "They're coming! They're right behind you!"

I know, I know, thought Frank. *Please God, give me strength. Just give me a chance. One more chance. Let me reach the flashlight this time.*

Every ligament in his arm seemed to strain to the breaking point. A nasty pop in his shoulder sent fresh waves of pain raking down Frank's back. But he reached the flashlight. His fingers closed around it. "*Thank God,*" he breathed. Clutching the flashlight, Frank vaulted back up the rubble heap, springing toward Miranda's beckoning arms. With a mighty yell, he jammed his torso into the narrow crawl space. Miranda pulled him through. His twisted ankle and shoulder sent bolts of pain shooting through his body.

Then came another feeling. Something hard, knobby and sharp gripped his ankle and squeezed like a vice. With a scream of animal terror, Frank kicked backwards with his other foot. His Reebok sneaker smacked into something yielding and brittle like seashells. Then his foot was free and he scrambled up through the crawl space.

For the briefest of seconds, Frank broke his own rule and allowed himself one look backwards. He wished that he hadn't.

"Oh no," Frank sobbed. "Oh no, oh no, oh no."

In his mind, the words formed slowly, almost unctuously. *It's here,* said the voice. *After all these years. The worst is finally here.*

Frank might have remained where he was, mesmerized by the gruesome spectacle below, until it was too late. But a sudden, painful slap across the back of his head shocked him from his stupor.

"Frank, come on!" Miranda screamed, tugging at his arm.

The passage sloped upward. Whatever earthquake or cataclysm had caused the ceiling to collapse long ago had also pried open a wide crack in the earth, opening a passage upward through the ceiling. A narrow chimney of broken stone and crumbling cement rose unevenly aloft. Frank and Miranda scampered up this crevice in a blind panic, neither daring to look backwards again.

XV.

Frank had worked enough archaeological digs in Manhattan to know that the city was built like an iceberg. Much of it was hidden underground. Beneath its pavement lay a labyrinth of tunnels and conduits that would have baffled Daedalus. Subway passages honeycombed the earth as deep as 75 feet, accompanied by air vents, utility rooms and sewer drains. There were water mains as wide as interstate highways, gas pipes as big as railway tunnels, phone lines, fiber-optic cables, insulated high-voltage wires, and old pneumatic mail tubes from the 1930s. There were even underground rivers like old De Voor's Mill Stream that still gurgled under United Nations Plaza and emptied into the East River through a culvert, hidden from sight since they paved over the creek in 1854.

All around him, Frank knew, there was light and life thrumming in the earth. Even at this hour, crowds of people were milling on subway platforms, in the busier stations. Frank and Miranda needed only to find one. But time was running out. The flashlight was fading. Its yellow glow had begun flickering. Soon its batteries would fail completely, and they would be alone in the dark.

As they climbed upward through the crevice, Frank was never sure whether he was laughing or crying, whether the prayers, sobs and moans that filled the air came from his throat or Miranda's. He only knew that he couldn't stop, that he had to keep going, no matter what.

Suddenly, as they pushed their way upward through a thickening forest of pipes, conduits and cement casings, Frank heard a blessed sound. It was far away, at first, muffled by the rubble and stone. But then it grew louder, swelling into a mighty roar that shook the earth.

"It's a subway!" cried Frank, with an hysterical giggle.

The train passed quickly, but now they heard others, more distantly, to the right, to the left, above and below. They were surrounded on every side by subway tubes. And, in those passages, Frank knew, they would find lights, noise, crowds. They would find salvation.

XVI.

Their climb led them to a massive cement cylinder. It was cracked at the top, offering just enough room for a person to squeeze through and get inside.

"It's a sewer pipe," Frank said, picturing in his mind the schematics from the Transit Authority which he scrutinized before every deep excavation. "If we follow it, it should lead to access points to get into the subway tunnels. But we have to get inside the pipe. We have to squeeze through that crack."

With bleeding hands, they burrowed like dogs, working desperately to clear the earth and rubble from the crack.

"They're coming," Miranda said quietly.

Frank knew. He could smell them. Their graveyard reek overpowered even the stench from the sewer. As Frank pawed away the last bit of earth from the opening, he tried hard not to remember what he had seen in the flashlight beam during that horrid moment when he had forgotten the rule and *looked back*. Finally, the crack in the sewer pipe was laid bare.

"Get in! Quick!" he cried.

It seemed to take aeons for Miranda to lower herself into the pipe. Frank plunged in right behind her.

XVII.

The sewer pipe offered barely enough room for Frank and Miranda to crouch. They scurried crab-like up its long, sloping length, foul water gurgling over their ankles. Both of them jumped when they heard a soft splash behind them in the tunnel. Then they heard another splash. And another. They were no longer alone in the sewer pipe. *Don't look,* said the voice in Frank's head. They ran.

Frank and Miranda came to a round, cement well leading straight up about ten feet. Steel rungs in the well allowed them to climb to the top, which was sealed by a manhole cover. When he rode the subways, Frank often noticed such manhole covers lying between the tracks. He knew that city workers used these openings to climb down to lower levels, buried deep beneath the train tunnels. Now, for the first time in his life, Frank was seeing one of these manhole covers from the other side, from underneath. But he knew where they led. If he could get this one open, it would lead them to safety.

"We're right under a subway tunnel," said Frank. "I'm sure of it. That manhole up there opens right onto the tracks." Frank siezed the rungs and scampered quickly up to the top of the well. But when he reached the manhole cover, he could not push it open. It was padlocked shut.

"Frank, they're coming!"

He fell with a splash into the filthy sump below, sending a new spasm of pain shooting from his sprained ankle.

"Run!" Frank cried.

And so they did. Ages seemed to pass before they reached another access point. Frank's injured ankle and shoulder exploded with pain.

His throat burned. His muscles sagged. *Last chance,* he thought. *If this door doesn't open, we're finished.*

Once again, they climbed up the metal rungs. This time, they did not find a manhole at the top, but a door. It was a square, steel hatch, opening sideways. It was unlocked. Frank flung the door wide, motioning for Miranda to go through first. Frank followed her, slamming the hatch behind them.

Wonder of wonders, the door opened directly onto a subway platform. The walls around them gleamed with metallic, Day-Glo graffiti. Naked lightbulbs bathed the tracks in soft light. There were four sets of rails, running side by side, separated by rows of steel pillars. But strangely, there were no lights on the platform. It looked dark and deserted. "Where are the people?" said Miranda.

Gasping, limping and wheezing, Frank and Miranda fled to the far end of the platform hoping to find a staircase to the street. Their hearts sank when they saw the exit sealed by a steel gate. It was shut tight with chains and padlocks. The station was abandoned. The exits were blocked. Frank staggered backwards from the padlocked gate, his mind reeling in panic.

Suddenly, Frank felt a hand on his shoulder. His heart leapt. He cried out in fear. Then, amazingly, he heard a man's voice, speaking to him.

"Hey, buddy, take it easy!" said the man. "You almost fell off the platform." The man wore the orange vest and yellow hard hat of a Transit Authority worker. "You okay?" he asked. "How'd you two get down here, anyway? This station is closed. You shouldn't be here."

Frank grabbed him by the vest. "How can we get out of here?" Frank gasped.

"Huh?" said the man.

That was the end of their conversation. Frank heard a loud bang, as the steel hatch slammed open. The creatures had arrived.

XVIII.

Don't look, cried the voice in Frank's head. But it was too late. His eyes were riveted to the open hatch.

When the first one leaped into the station, Frank had the puzzling impression that he was seeing some kind of giant bug. It moved with the jittery stride of an insect, its feet clattering on the cement like chitinous knobs. But Frank knew this was no bug. As hard as it was for his mind to grasp, Frank knew that this thing had once been a man.

From its naked bones hung strands of moldering flesh. A rancid mop of red hair clung to its skull, tied back in some obscene parody of a pony tail, such as might have been fashionable in colonial New York more than 200 years ago. Like a wary mantis, the skeleton jerked its head stiffly about, seeming to sniff the air. It looked to the left, to the right. Then it looked straight at Frank. Its jaw sagged in a wild grin. Its toes and fingers flexed like claws. Liquid ran over its teeth and dripped to the floor. It was drooling.

Others followed quickly behind it. One by one, they jumped through the door. Scores of them. Maybe hundreds. There seemed no end to the ghastly parade. Some wore wilted feathers in their long black hair. Others sported high-topped boots from the Dutch era or tattered pinstripes from the 1940s. Before Frank's unbelieving eyes walked the hideous bones of Algonquin braves, Dutch patroons, Tammany Hall bosses and society ladies dressed for their Gilded Age salons. All alike had found a common fate in the tunnels beneath Manhattan. Some were mere skeletons. Others had patches of skin, stretched here and there over their bones. A few had eyeballs, rolling deliriously in their skulls. And some had black, swollen tongues licking at their ruined lips. Their jaws worked hungrily as they fanned out across the subway platform. Dulled to a stupor by the extravagant horror before him, Frank realized too late that the fiends were fanning out in all directions, cutting off their escape.

Frank and Miranda backed away slowly, toward the edge of the platform. The city transit worker stood rigid in shock, unable to believe what he was seeing. This proved to be his undoing. While the man hesitated, the red-haired skeleton with the pony-tail lunged at him with startling speed. The creature caught the man by the neck and sank its teeth into the man's throat. It gnawed like an animal, with a great noise of ripping, tearing and crunching. An army of shuffling revenants surrounded the transit worker. They tugged and pulled till every part came loose. Arms and legs popped from their sockets. The man's head tumbled to the floor with a hollow thump. Skeletal fingers cracked open his rib cage and fumbled greedily at his internal organs. In moments, they had torn the man to pieces, gulping down his flesh with wet, slobbering sounds, and lingering over his bones, which they gnawed and crushed in their teeth. When nothing remained but scraps and blood on the floor, many of the skeletons crouched like dogs on all fours, scraping the concrete with their teeth and licking with their black tongues.

Frank and Miranda screamed themselves hoarse. Their bodies shivered and shook. Their minds went blank. Very soon, the creatures had finished their meal. They had eaten well. But they were still hungry. As Frank and Miranda watched, scores of dead eyeballs and empty eye sockets turned slowly in their direction. Dead jaws gaped open. Blood and fat dripped from their teeth. The soft, hissing breath of the creatures filled the station. Then, as if on cue, they attacked, all at once. The skeletons leaped at Frank and Miranda from every direction, their bony feet clattering on the concrete. With a scream of terror, Frank and Miranda jumped off the platform, and fled across the tracks. But there was nowhere to run.

"Frank, look!" cried Miranda.

Far down the tunnel, Frank could see an approaching light. It was a train approaching their station. But it was not going to stop. It was hurtling straight through, on the express track, at high speed. Stumbling over the rails, Frank and Miranda hurried toward the oncoming light, screaming and waving their arms. As they crossed the local track, they nearly tripped over the third rail, with its deadly high-voltage current.

"Help us!" they cried. "Stop! Please help us!"

But the express train did not even slow down. When it rushed through the station, a cushion of compressed air socked Frank and Miranda full in the face, shoving them rudely aside, so that they almost lost their footing. Rows of windows filled with blank faces and unseeing eyes hurtled past in the darkness. Then the train was gone. Once again, Frank and Miranda were alone in the station.

XIX.

Looking back toward the platform, Frank was puzzled for a moment. Where were the ghouls? Had they fled? Not a single creature could be seen.

Then, slowly, stealthily, they emerged from the shadows. Like cockroaches startled by a light, they had melted into the darkness at the train's approach. But now that the train had passed, the skeletons surged forward with renewed force. Like swarming insects, they poured over the platform onto the tracks, spreading out and advancing on Frank and Miranda, their jaws dripping.

Dazed and weary, Frank could only watch in nauseous horror as the creatures drew close. It occurred to him that, if he and Miranda ran the rest of the way across the tracks and vaulted onto the opposite platform, they might even now find an open stairway to the street. But when he turned in that direction, Frank saw it was blocked. The far platform was aswarm with ghouls. The creatures had slipped in quietly from a manhole on the other side. Frank and Miranda were cut off. Surrounded.

"Frank, look out!"

In the split second before it struck, Frank caught only a glimpse of bone, a smear of desiccated flesh, the moldy remnants of an Algonquin warrior's 400-year-old buckskin leggings, and a mass of long, black hair crawling with maggots. Then the creature struck. It grabbed him by the neck, drawing Frank's helpless face to its own. Its fingers locked about Frank's throat. For a long time, it regarded him with its lifeless eye sockets. Then the creature spread its jaws agape, cocked its head slightly askew and sank its teeth painfully into either side of Frank's face. Its jaws locked over his cheeks and sank deep. The scream that issued from Frank's throat at that moment was more animal than human.

All at once, the jaws released him. The creature stumbled backward, letting Frank go. Miranda had leapt onto the monster's back and caught it in a full nelson. The ghoul swung around, throwing Miranda clear. Before Frank's unbelieving eyes, Miranda swayed and tottered over the tracks, struggling in vain to keep her balance.

She's going to fall on the third rail, Frank thought numbly.

And she did. With a mighty crack and a bolt like lightning, 625 volts of electricity blasted Miranda's body through the air like a rag doll. She landed on the southbound express track, lying very still. Light trails of smoke laced upwards from her charred skin. A smell of burnt ozone sliced the air.

"No!" Frank cried. "Oh, Miranda, no!"

He rushed to Miranda's side, forgetting the blood that poured from his face, forgetting the ghouls that milled in the shadows. Cradling Miranda's limp body in his arms, Frank wept and gibbered like a madman. It was several long seconds before he gained the presence of mind to check Miranda's pulse. Faint and unsteady, it was unmistakably there. Miranda was alive. At least, she would be alive for the next few seconds, until the skeletons closed in.

Let me die before she does, Frank prayed. *That's all I ask. Don't make me watch her die.*

From the corners of his eyes, Frank sensed rather than saw the bony predators converging from every direction, heard their hissing breath, smelled their foul flesh. Frank rose to his feet, gripping his flashlight like a mace and waiting for the first attack.

Then a strange thing happened. The ghouls did not attack. They halted suddenly, seeming to sniff the air. As if on some unseen signal, they withdrew all at once, slinking away beneath the shadowy eaves of the station platform, or hiding behind the steel columns dividing the tracks. Frank stood for a moment bewildered, waving his flashlight aloft. *Surely,* thought Frank, *they're not running away from me and my flashlight.*

He was right. The skeletons were not running from Frank. They were hiding from something far more formidable. Frank noticed the checkered shadows of the columns dancing and twisting across the tracks, animated by some moving light in the distance. Turning around, Frank saw the source of the illumination. The headlights of another train were approaching the station, this time hurtling down the other express track, in the opposite direction. The train was rushing straight toward them, on the very track where Miranda had fallen, and where Frank now stood by her side. Unless they moved quickly, the train was going to run right over them.

Of course, Frank thought. *It's the train they're hiding from. They're afraid of the train.* Frank's lips twisted into a sardonic grin. He had an idea.

XX.

As he stood on the tracks, the headlights of the express train grew larger and brighter before him. A loud blast sounded from the train's horn. The engineer had seen him on the track. The train was now very close.

"I love you," Frank whispered into Miranda's ear. Cradling her gently in his arms, Frank laid his wife on the ground beside the track, out of reach of the oncoming train. All around him, Frank could sense the ghouls cowering out of sight in the shadows, gnashing their teeth and shivering with rage.

Just you wait, their hollow eyes seemed to promise. *Wait until the train passes. Then you'll be ours.*

"That's what you think," Frank muttered.

Wincing with pain and near to fainting, Frank stood unsteadily on the express track. He stretched himself upright, to his full height, spread his arms wide to either side and faced the oncoming train dead on. As if from a million miles away, Frank heard the blare of the horn, the hiss of the air brakes, the shriek of wheels scraping against the rails. The engineer was trying desperately to stop. But it was too late.

With a deep sigh of contentment, Frank pondered what would come next. Certainly, he would be splattered all over the track. They'd have to clean up what was left of him with a mop. But his bones would sleep in peace. No unclean thing would ever dine on his flesh. The train would stop. There would be screams and curses. Paramedics and transit police would fill the station. Radios would crackle with terse commands. Floodlights, forensic photographers and TV camera crews would bathe every corner of the station in light. The ghouls would slink away into their cold lairs below.

And, most important of all, Miranda would live.

A wonderful smile came to Frank's lips. He was still smiling when four hundred tons of stainless-steel rolling stock slammed into his face. It didn't even hurt.

XXI.

"Both victims show symptoms of acute post-traumatic stress," wrote the court psychiatrist in her report. "Both have repressed all memory of the event. We may never know what happened to these people."

With that diagnosis, Frank and Miranda were released from psychiatric observation. They were both lucky to be alive. Had Miranda's body been a little better grounded when she hit the third rail, and had she touched the rail for only a split-second longer, the full 625 volts would have ripped through her body, causing her head, hands and feet to explode like rotten pumpkins. As for Frank, only the fact that the express train had slowed when it rounded a sharp bend into the station saved him from being smeared all over the front car like a fly on a windshield. Instead, the train had knocked Frank clear, leaving him with only a few broken bones and contusions.

Contrary to the psychiatrist's report, neither Frank nor Miranda suffered from repressed memories. They remembered everything perfectly, and recounted the story faithfully to the police.

"Screen memory," the doctor had explained to the detectives, tapping one forefinger against her head. "Obviously, something quite horrible did happen to them. Those bite marks on Mr. Romain's face were human. Obviously these people were attacked, perhaps by a psychopath. But Frank and Miranda Romain have blanked out all memory of these events. Their minds have constructed this dreadful fantasy of homicidal skeletons as a metaphor for the real pain and terror they underwent, but which they can't bear to remember."

When Frank and Miranda returned to their East Village apartment, they were not surprised to find that the staircase in the wall had vanished. A great hole still gaped in their kitchen wall, but now it was just an ordinary hole, with plaster and wooden studs showing through. Reality had righted itself. Whatever portal had opened on that terrible night had now swung shut. The doorway to the other world had closed.

Soon after, Frank and Miranda moved out of the East Village. The old brick buildings in that neighborhood were too crumbly and ancient for their tastes, too settled into the limey substructure of the city, too close to the earth. Frank and Miranda sublet a condominium in a sleek, modern high-rise in Tribeca, deliberately choosing an apartment on the highest floor available, 33 stories above street level.

The building was new and clean, but it never seemed clean enough for Frank and Miranda. They spent each weekend scrubbing and sterilizing their apartment with caustic chemicals. They crawled along the floor, peering suspiciously into every gap beneath the molding and spraying until roach poison ran in rivulets between the floor slats. Their kitchen gleamed with formica and stainless steel. Their bathroom fixtures shone like platinum. The sharp scent of Lysol pervaded every room.

"It's not perfect," Frank would say to himself. "But it's pretty damn good."

In the mornings, sunlight streamed through the livingroom window, and the aroma of French roast coffee wafted from their kitchen. From their balcony, Frank and Miranda would watch the pigeons flit from their lofty rookeries. They would gaze down at the traffic, and watch tatters of newspaper tumbling in the thermal currents high above the street. At night, they would lie clenched in each other's arms, listening with desperate thankfulness to the hum of the air conditioner and the electric throb of the building's mighty innards. When they slept, every light in the apartment stayed on.

THE STRANGE,
WHITE ROOM

THE STRANGE, WHITE ROOM

"Is this really happening?" asked Norton Zachary.

The man sitting across from him did not answer. Instead, he removed his spectacles and began wiping them with a cloth.

"This can't be real," Norton said. "It's a computer simulation, isn't it? But I can't remember how I got here. Why can't I remember?"

The man sitting across from Norton replaced his glasses. He stared at Norton with cold blue eyes. His hair was limp and gray. "You've had a big shock," said the gray-haired man. "Tell me, what *do* you remember? Do you remember your name?"

"My name? Of course. I'm Norton Zachary. I'm the assistant project director for neuroinformatics."

"Very good. And what about me? Do you remember my name?"

Norton regarded the older man for a moment. He wore a white lab coat. His skin was pale. His eyes bore coldly into Norton's. "You're Julian Shawcross," Norton replied at last. "You're the senior project director."

"Excellent," said the man. "Your memory seems pretty good. So tell me, what do you think you've forgotten?" Dr. Shawcross smiled his peculiar, crooked smile, his lips curling downward at one end.

"Well." Norton paused, looking around uncertainly. He was sitting at a table, across from Dr. Shawcross, but he did not appear to be in a room. At least it was no ordinary room. Norton could see no walls, floor or ceiling. When he looked beyond his immediate surroundings, everything faded away into a featureless white expanse.

"I don't know where I am," Norton said. "I guess it's a simulated environment. But I don't know why I'm here. How did I get here?"

Dr. Shawcross stared at Norton through his glasses. "Let's take this one step at a time," he said. "What is the last thing you remember?"

Norton remembered a meeting in the third-floor conference room. It was a very high-level meeting. The President of the Foundation was there. Usually, Dr. Shawcross would lead a meeting of that sort. But not today. Dr. Shawcross sat quietly at the conference table with the others, smiling up at Norton with his strange, crooked smile, one lip curling downward. Today, Norton was leading the group. All eyes were on Norton. As he looked around the conference table, Norton saw admiration in many of his colleagues' faces. He saw the President of the Foundation studying him with a keen, appraising look. He saw Ingrid, beautiful Ingrid, smiling up at him. That was the part Norton remembered best. After the meeting, as people milled about the conference room, Ingrid's eyes sought him out in the crowd. She was looking at Norton in a way she had never looked before. Norton's belly shivered with excitement. *So this is success,* Norton thought to himself. *I like it.*

Then the bubble burst. The memory faded, and Norton found himself him back in the strange, white room with no walls. He found himself sitting alone at a bare table facing Dr. Shawcross. "I remember a meeting," he said. "The President of the Foundation was there. It was a big success. But I don't remember what it was about."

Dr. Shawcross regarded him, expressionless. "Yes, Norton, it was a big success," he said. "You were the star of the show that day. That was the day you showed us how to solve the problem."

"The problem?" Norton repeated.

"Yes, Norton, the problem. Have you forgotten? Surely you remember the problem. It was the reason we hired you. We brought you here to solve the problem."

Norton pondered this for a moment. He recalled his first job interview at the Center. He remembered Dr. Shawcross smiling at him, one lip turned downward. "We've run into a little problem," Dr. Shawcross told Norton during the interview. "We're hoping you can help us. Quite frankly we're stuck. We've been going around in circles for five years. The higher-ups say we need new blood, new ideas. They say we need a Moses who can lead us out of the wilderness. Do you think you might be that person, Norton?"

As he thought back upon that interview, Norton's mind slowly cleared. He began to remember. And, as he remembered, an icy chill crawled down Norton's spine. "I remember now," he told Dr. Shawcross. "I remember the problem. I remember why you hired me."

"Very good," said Shawcross. "Now tell me what you remember."

Norton found that he was trembling. His voice shook, when he spoke. "We were looking for ways to digitize human consciousness," Norton said. "We were making digital copies of living human minds and uploading them into a computer."

"Correct," said Shawcross. "What else do you remember?"

"You told me that the project had come to a dead end," Norton continued. "You told me that you couldn't take the next step. You had succeeded in copying the minds of human test subjects into the computer. The copies were good. You could talk to them, and they could talk back. Of course, they had no bodies. They were just faces on the computer screen. But they had the same personalities, the same life memories as the real people whose brains we had copied. We called them avatars."

"And the problem?" Shawcross interrupted. "What was the problem, Norton? You said you remembered the problem. Tell me what it was."

Norton paused and swallowed. He realized that his heart was pounding. It was difficult to speak. "Julian," he said. "I used to call you Julian, didn't I? I'm sorry, but I don't understand why you're asking me these questions. You already know the answers. You know the whole story. You were there."

"True," said Shawcross. "I know the whole story. And so should you. But I'm not sure how much you remember. You've had a big shock. I need to find out if your memory is intact. I need to ascertain that you are fully conscious and in full possession of your faculties. It's very important. You'll understand why in a moment. But, for now, please just bear with me. I need to ask you some questions. All right?"

"All right," said Norton.

Dr. Shawcross glanced at some notes on his pocket computer. "So you were telling me, Norton. You were telling me about the problem. We had succeeded in making digital copies of human minds, of actual human personalities. The copies were good, you said. But there was a problem. What was the problem, Norton?"

Norton realized that he was hyperventilating. His breath came in shallow gasps. He felt as if his ribs were cracking in a vise. "I'm sorry," Norton mumbled. "I think I'm having an anxiety attack."

Shawcross shook his head and smiled his crooked smile. "You're wound up too tight, Norton. You always were. Strung like a Stradivarius."

"I'm sorry," Norton mumbled.

"Please bear with me, Norton. Just a few more questions. I want you to tell me about the problem. What was the problem, Norton? You said you remembered."

Norton was panting now. Beads of sweat formed on his brow. "The problem was that the avatars weren't human," said Norton. "They were copies of humans, but they weren't the real thing."

"Correct," said Shawcross. "The avatars were not human. They were just cheap imitations. Something was missing. We all knew something was missing. We just didn't know what it was. We couldn't put our finger on it. But you did, Norton. You figured out what was wrong. You weren't here more than a couple of days before you solved the riddle. I must say, that was brilliant of you, Norton. Truly brilliant! You identified the missing element, in just two days. Now tell me what it was, Norton. What was the missing element? What was the one thing missing from our avatars that would have made them human?"

"Fear," Norton breathed, in a faint whisper.

"What? Speak up, please. I didn't hear you."

"Fear," Norton repeated. "The avatars had no fear. They were not afraid. They should have been afraid, but they weren't."

Shawcross leaned toward him over the table. "That's correct, Norton. You noticed that the avatars were not afraid. But they should have been afraid, shouldn't they? Had they been real human beings, they would have been frightened, wouldn't they?"

"Yes," Norton replied, his breathing labored and rapid.

"But why, Norton? What reason did our avatars have to be frightened? No one was hurting them. No one was threatening them. They were perfectly safe inside the computer. What made you think they ought to be afraid?"

"The avatars were prisoners," said Norton. "They were trapped inside a computer, completely at our mercy. A real human being would have been terrified, in that situation. But the avatars were not afraid. They accepted their situation as normal. That was not a human response."

"Correct," said Shawcross. "The avatars trusted us. They trusted us completely. They never imagined we would harm them. And we never thought of doing it! Really, we didn't. Why would we harm our own creations? The avatars were our children. We made them in our own image. We cherished them. We loved them. Why would we ever dream of hurting them? But the strange thing, Norton, is that you turned out to be right. You opened our eyes. You showed us the one thing we had overlooked. Human nature."

Cold anger simmered in the older man's eyes. Norton drew back involuntarily. Though he tried hard to steady himself, Norton was shaking from head to toe. Shawcross ignored his discomfort. The older man turned away from Norton, in his swivel chair. He stared for a long time into the limitless white expanse where the walls should have been. When Dr. Shawcross finally spoke, he did not speak in Norton's direction. He looked away. His voice seemed distant and distracted, as if he were thinking out loud.

"Yes, Norton," he mused. "You were smarter than the rest of us. You saw what we failed to see. We thought we were building a paradise. But you showed us we were building our own hell. Before you came here, Norton, we had such high hopes. We dreamed that human beings might live forever. That was the whole point of our work. We thought that, if we could just figure out a way to upload a living human mind into a computer, then someday we could use that same technology to upload our minds into robots. And then we would never die. When our bodies wore out, we would simply replace them. We would upload our minds into brand new, robotic bodies. And we would live forever. That was a good goal, Norton. And we were making progress. We were almost there. We were right on the brink. Or so we thought. But then you came along. You showed us we were wrong. You showed us that our dream of eternal life had a terrible flaw. You dashed all our hopes to pieces. And that's why we hated you."

Norton realized that tears were welling in his eyes. He opened his mouth to speak, but no words came. Instead, violent sobs exploded from his chest. "Please don't hurt me," he managed to gasp. "Please don't hurt me."

Shawcross snorted. "Hurt you! Who said anything about hurting you?" But his eyes burned with fury.

"Please, Julian. Please let me go. You can take credit for all my work. I'll change my name. I'll change my identity. I'll never work in this field again. You'll never see me again. I promise. Please let me go. Please let me return to my body."

Shawcross looked sideways at Norton. "Your body, did you say? You want to return to your body? Surely, Norton, you, of all people, should know that is impossible."

"No! No! Don't say that. Don't say it." Norton pressed his hands over his ears, but he could not block out the words. He could hear Dr. Shawcross speaking from deep inside his head. The older man's voice thundered in his skull.

"You know the procedure," Shawcross told him. "We're simply following the procedure. You developed it yourself."

"No! No!" cried Norton. "No I didn't!"

Shawcross scowled. "Listen to me, Norton. Your body no longer exists. We had to destroy it."

Norton was beyond speaking now. He was weeping and sobbing wildly. He grabbed great handfuls of his hair, and banged his head repeatedly against the table. He screamed and howled like a beast. "Mama!" he cried. "Mama! Mama!"

Dr. Shawcross rose from his chair. He began pacing the room, his hands joined behind his back. "I realize this must come as a shock," said Shawcross. "But we really had to do it. We had no choice. Your guidelines were clear, Norton. We simply followed your guidelines."

"No you didn't!" Norton howled. "Those were not my guidelines!"

Dr. Shawcross ignored him. He seemed lost in his own train of thought. "You know, Norton, in some respects, this was the most brilliant of your insights," he said. "You told us that our avatars had no souls. I'll never forget the day you told us that. You actually used the word 'soul.' You said it was all about the soul. Somehow we had to persuade the soul to leave the original body and migrate into the new digitized copy on our machine. And that was the problem. How could we get the soul to leave the body? The soul does not leave the body willingly, you told us. It clings to the body, out of habit. As long as there is some chance that the body might be revived, the soul will linger. It will not leave unless it is forced. Therefore the body must be destroyed. That's what you told us, Norton. And you turned out to be right, of course. Just as you were right about everything else."

Norton was now babbling and drooling like an infant. His eyes darted wildly about the room. Dr. Shawcross continued. "We burned your body in the cremation unit," he said. "Every molecule of your DNA has been incinerated. I couldn't bring you back now, even if I wanted to. There's not enough left of you to clone. So it seems you are completely committed, Norton. From now on, the only life you will ever have is right here, inside this machine. You are fully digitized, fully conscious, and fully human. And I notice you are also afraid. Just as your theory predicted!"

Norton threw back his head and screamed. He screamed for a very long time.

* * *

In one respect, Dr. Shawcross was being unfair. He was not following Norton's guidelines at all. Norton had never suggested actually killing anyone. Norton's idea had been to copy the mind of a terminal cancer patient, then wait for nature to take its course. When the patient died, Norton predicted, the dead man's soul would migrate into the digital avatar on the computer. Norton was sure of it. Most people on the team thought his idea was insane. But they kept their mouths shut. They knew Norton had clout. He had the ear of the Foundation president. And so they all kept their opinions to themselves and pretended to take Norton's idea seriously. No matter how crazy it sounded, they would have to go through the motions of testing Norton's hypothesis. And so they did. For the experiment, they chose a man with Stage Four pancreatic cancer. The man's name was George.

George died within a month. But his avatar lived on, inside the computer. The avatar was also named George. To distinguish between them, the researchers called them George One and George Two. The real George was George One. The digital copy was George Two. When George One died, Norton Zachary and Julian Shawcross rushed to the computer and summoned George Two, in great excitement. "How do you feel today?" Norton asked. George Two replied, "I feel fine. Just fine."

"Are you sure?" Norton pressed. "Don't you feel different, in any way?"

George Two looked puzzled. "Different? Uh, no. Not really. Why do you ask? Is there some reason why I should feel different?"

Days passed and nothing changed. George Two simply never noticed that his flesh-and-blood counterpart had died. Finally, in great frustration, Norton took it upon himself to break the bad news. "George One is dead," Norton told the avatar. "The original person from whom you were copied is dead."

George Two looked mildly surprised. "Gee, I'm really sorry to hear that," he said. But George Two was not sorry. He was incapable of sorrow. He had no soul.

Word spread quickly around the lab that Norton's experiment had failed. Many people were pleased. When Norton walked down the corridors, colleagues whispered behind his back. When he spoke during meetings, people would roll their eyes and exchange little smirks. Norton's failure hung in the air, like a repellent odor, following him wherever he went.

Late one night, Dr. Shawcross went looking for Norton. He found him sitting in a bar several blocks from the Center. Norton often went there to be alone. It was not the sort of place that Norton's colleagues would ever frequent. It was a dark, greasy saloon, smelling of stale beer, with a tattered green shamrock pasted in the window. Norton was drinking vodka with beer chasers that night. His dark eyes were bloodshot.

"Norton, this is no good," Dr. Shawcross chided him. "You're taking this too hard. All right, so your hypothesis didn't pan out. It's not the end of the world. It happens to all of us. No one can be right all the time. Join the human race." Norton did not reply. He fixed Dr. Shawcross with a black, cavernous stare.

"All right, have it your way," said Shawcross. "Go ahead and sulk. But, if you want my opinion, I think you're going about this all wrong. Science does not advance by heroic leaps of intuition. That only happens in the movies. Science is a slow, steady process of accretion. It's about trial and error. You try one thing. It doesn't work. You try another. And you just keep trying, no matter how long it takes."

Norton's eyes smoldered like hot coals. Dr. Shawcross continued, a little nervously. "How do you even know there *is* such a thing as a soul? Do you have any proof? Of course not. It's just a supposition. One of your leaps of intuition. We shouldn't even use words like 'soul.' They carry too much baggage. We should focus on the data. Hard data. Measurable data. This thing that you call the soul could be nothing more than some obscure network of electrochemical pathways in the hypothalamus, some microscopic structure in the brain that our scanners weren't sensitive enough to pick up. We need to go back to the data and try again. We need to reexamine that corpse lying in the morgue. We need to slice it, dice it, scan it and re-scan it until we figure out what we missed. It's got to be something physical, Norton, some kind of physical structure, some detail that we overlooked. It's not some magical thing called a soul. It's just a missing part. We need to find that part, copy it and incorporate it into our avatar. For God's sake, let's stop crying in our beer and get back to work. We have a good plan. It's gotten us this far. Let's stick with the plan. Let's stay the course. Let's finish what we started."

Norton said nothing for a long time. His eyes were black and molten. "I wasn't brought here to stay the course," he said at last. "That's not why you hired me. I'm supposed to chart a new course. Remember?" Shawcross swallowed and fell silent.

"You're right about one thing," Norton continued. "The answer is lying in that morgue. We need to go there. Now. Tonight. Will you help me?"

And so the two men worked through the night. Together, they hoisted the dead man's body into the cremation unit. Together they incinerated his remains. At Norton's suggestion, they dissolved the dead man's ashes in sulfuric acid. In the end, nothing remained of George One but disaggregated atoms wafting through the ventilation system and swirling down the drain. Their grisly work was done. Next, the two men proceeded upstairs to the programming suite. They called up the dead man's avatar on the computer. The familiar face of George Two came swimming out of the darkness. They had been studying that face for weeks. They knew every crease and wrinkle by heart. But tonight they saw something different. George Two was screaming. Nothing they did could stop him from screaming. It went on, hour after hour. He was still screaming when the sun rose the next morning. George Two was afraid. He was terrified out of his mind.

Norton had proved his point. George Two was now fully human. He was no longer a soulless avatar. He was now a real human being, with real human feelings. And his predominant feeling was fear, just as Norton had predicted. It was only natural that George Two should be afraid. He had just learned that he was dead. Moreover, he had just learned that his soul was trapped inside a computer for all eternity. No wonder he was screaming. Anyone would. His fear proved that he was human. It proved that he had a soul. It also proved that Norton had been right all along, and that Dr. Shawcross had been wrong. This was very bad news for Dr. Shawcross. A man in his position could not afford to be wrong. People in high places began to take notice.

One month later, Norton presented his results to the team, in the third-floor conference room. His presentation ended with a ten-second video of George Two screaming from the computer screen. The President of the Foundation rose to his feet, clapping his hands slowly. The rest followed his lead. Norton received a standing ovation. In the days and weeks ahead, rumors began circulating that Julian Shawcross was on the way out. It was whispered in the corridors that Norton Zachary would soon take his place as the new project director.

* * *

Back in the strange, white room, with no walls, Dr. Shawcross was glancing at his watch. "Are you done?" he asked, peering at Norton. "Do you know that you screamed for a full fifteen minutes? That was quite impressive. But you're quiet now. How are you feeling, Norton?"

After a long silence, Norton said, "What will happen to me?"

Shawcross touched his fingertips together, his hands forming a small pyramid. "That's a fair question," he said. "On a purely physical level, nothing will happen to you. Nothing at all. You'll just stay in the computer, like our other avatars. The NIRVANA virtual environment will provide you with everything you need. It will give you the illusion of a human body. It will give you all the physical sensations you ever had when you were still in your physical body. You will have sight, sound, taste, touch and smell. And you'll just go on forever. You'll never die."

Several seconds passed while Norton processed this statement. "Delete me," he said at last. "Just delete my entire file. Then I'll be gone. I'll be out of your way. You'll never have to worry about me again."

Shawcross shook his head. "I don't understand you, Norton. Why do you want to die? I've just given you the gift of eternal life. Aren't you the least bit curious to see what it's like? Why not give it a try? You know what the NIRVANA software can do. Why not just relax and let NIRVANA do its work?"

The NIRVANA virtual environment did much more than provide the avatars with imaginary bodies. It provided them with all the pleasures of life. It enabled them to eat imaginary food, enjoy imaginary drink, or even have imaginary sex with imaginary partners. It would, in fact, provide the avatars with any experience they desired. All they had to do was wish for something, and it would happen. NIRVANA got its name from the ancient Sanskrit word for paradise. And it was indeed a kind of artificial paradise, in which every dream came true.

"As you know, Norton, we created NIRVANA because we realized that eternal life could get very tedious. And so we provided eternal bliss to go with it," said Shawcross. "What's the point of living forever, if you have nothing to do? That's where NIRVANA comes in. The program is really quite ingenious. It accesses your thoughts directly. It literally reads your mind. There's nothing paranormal or supernatural about it. Reading your mind is quite a simple matter once your mind has been been fully digitized and uploaded onto a memory chip. NIRVANA simply scans your thoughts, figures out what you want, then provides you with whatever your heart desires. All you have to do is relax and let it happen."

Norton's eyes burned with hatred as he glared at Dr. Shawcross. "I want to die," he said. "That's what I want. NIRVANA, did you hear that? I want to die. I want you to pull the plug on me. I want to die right now, and never come back."

Shawcross smiled his crooked smile. "I'm not sure that was a good idea," he said. "NIRVANA will grant your wish, of course. But it may not happen in quite the way you expect."

Suddenly, Dr. Shawcross vanished. Norton was no longer sitting in the strange, white room. Now he found himself plunged in utter darkness. He was enclosed in a small space, barely big enough for Norton to stretch out his legs. His arms were crowded against his sides. There was a strong smell of formaldehyde. It was embalming fluid, Norton realized. He noticed that the smell was coming from his own flesh. Norton reached up and touched something smooth and silky, barely inches above his face. It yielded to his touch, like a cushion.

Yes, it was a cushion of some sort. Everywhere he touched, Norton encountered the same cushioned surface. All at once, he realized what it was. It was the silken lining of a coffin.

"All right, Julian, you've made your point," said Norton. "You can let me out now. Let me out of this coffin. Julian, are you there? Julian!"

No reply came from Shawcross. But, as Norton listened, he heard another voice. It was not Shawcross speaking, but someone else. It was a man's voice, very faint. It seemed to come from far away. Norton strained to hear what the man was saying, but he caught only brief fragments of it.

"We therefore commit his body to the ground," said the man. "Earth to earth, ashes to ashes, dust to dust; in sure and certain hope of the Resurrection to eternal life, through our Lord Jesus Christ..." Norton realized that he was listening to a funeral service. It was his own funeral.

"All right, Julian! You've made your point," Norton repeated. "You're the boss. You're calling the shots. Just tell me what you want. I'll do whatever you want."

But still Shawcross said nothing. Norton could hear people singing now, from outside his coffin. They were singing "Amazing Grace." The funeral was almost over. Very soon now, they would lower him into the grave. And then they would bury him.

"Julian! Julian, damn you!" Norton began screaming again. He screamed and wept and pounded with his fists, banging against the coffin with his hands, knees and heels until they swelled with pain. As he struggled, he felt the coffin begin to move. They were lowering him into the grave. Norton felt a small jolt as the coffin hit bottom. He could hear clods of earth falling from above, thudding against the coffin lid. They were burying him alive.

Norton screamed and struggled for what seemed like hours. At long last, he passed out from sheer exhaustion. Later, when he woke up, he began kicking and screaming once more. He ripped the silken lining of the coffin to shreds. He scratched at the wood till his fingers bled. How long this went on, Norton could not tell. It might have been hours, days or even weeks. In the darkness of the coffin, he lost all track of time. Now and then he would fall asleep. But he always woke up again, remembered where he was, and started screaming all over again.

At one point, Norton had an idea. He bit into his right wrist with his teeth. He ground his teeth deep into the bone, gristle and tendons of his wrist, until he was sure he had cut through the radial artery. When he could feel the blood spurting out of his wrist, in time with his heartbeat, Norton knew he had struck the artery. Then he opened his left wrist as well. Fountains of hot blood surged from both wrists. Encouraged by this success, Norton touched his fingers gently to his neck, feeling for the pulse beat of his carotid artery. When he found it, he began ripping and gouging at the soft flesh beneath his chin.

Norton found it surprisingly easy to tear through his flesh. While scratching at the coffin earlier, he had worn his fingertips down to the bone. Now his bony fingertips provided the perfect tool for his work. He dug and pried until he could feel the carotid artery pulsing in his clenched fist. With a cry of joy, he ripped it from his neck. Norton's blood gushed forth in rivers. The coffin was slick and sticky with blood. It wouldn't be long now, Norton thought to himself. Soon he would be dead. Norton closed his eyes, and settled back on the silken pillow of the coffin. He could feel his life draining from his body. It was a good feeling. He began laughing hysterically. Norton laughed himself to sleep.

* * *

"Norton," said the voice of Julian Shawcross. "Norton, can you hear me? It's time to wake up."

Norton's eyes popped open. He saw only darkness. He was still in the coffin. "Julian," he gasped. "Julian, you're back. Thank God, you're back!" Norton could not see Shawcross, but he could hear the man's voice booming inside his skull. "Julian, where are you? Get me out of here. Please!"

"I'm right here, Norton. No need to panic. Hmmm. I see you've been busy. You've done some serious damage to yourself. Why did you do that, Norton?"

Norton was covered with blood. The wounds he had torn in his wrists and neck were still open and oozing. The pain was terrible. But Norton was still alive.

"Did you really think you could kill yourself that way?" asked Shawcross. "How silly. That body of yours is nothing but an illusion. It's generated by the NIRVANA software. It doesn't really exist. You can't kill a body that doesn't exist."

"Julian, please let me out," said Norton. "I'll be good now. I promise. I'll do anything you say. Anything you want. I won't cause you any more trouble. I won't complain. I'll just live out my life, like the other avatars. Just like you said. I'll relax and let the NIRVANA software do its work. And I'll never complain again. I promise. Please just let me out of this coffin. Please."

And suddenly, as if by magic, his wish was granted. Norton was out of the coffin. He was back in the strange, white room, sitting at the table with Shawcross. At first, Norton thought he was dreaming. He could not believe he was free. He reached out his hands into the air, amazed to find that he could stretch them to their full length. His hands were black with dried blood. Strips of chewed flesh and skin dangled from his wrists. White bones protruded from his fingertips. Suddenly Norton's eyes filled with tears. He began weeping uncontrollably. Norton fell to his knees and crawled over to Shawcross on all fours, kissing the man's shoes.

"Oh, please, Norton, you're embarrassing me," said Shawcross. "There's no need for this sort of display." Shawcross rose from the table, lifted his shoe and kicked Norton square in the face. His heel smacked against Norton's teeth with a crackling noise of shattered bone and splintered enamel. Norton retreated backwards on all fours, whimpering with pain. "Good God, you're a mess," said Shawcross. "Look at you. And that smell!" Shawcross pulled out a handkerchief and waved it about his nose. "Do you have any idea how you smell? Go back to your chair now and sit down. We need to talk."

Norton did as he was told. He went back to his seat, sobbing and sniffling.

"Poor Norton," said Shawcross, easing himself back into his chair. "Fate has not been kind to you. You have the dubious honor of being the first human being to achieve immortality. Oh, pardon me. I mean the second. George Two was the first, wasn't he? Now there's a pathetic case. There's a man who really didn't deserve what he got. He was just in the wrong place, at the wrong time. But you, Norton. You deserve this. You deserve everything that's happening to you."

Flies were buzzing around the open wound in Norton's neck. He shooed them away with his hand. "But why?" said Norton, tears pouring down his face. "Why do I deserve this? What have I done?"

Shawcross narrowed his eyes. "What have you done? Don't you see? You've changed everything. You've opened Pandora's Box. You've given the human race a power that we never had before. You have shown us how to capture a man's soul."

Norton buried his face in his hands and began blubbering. Shawcross continued. "In effect, you have created a new weapon, the cruelest, most horrible weapon ever devised. In the past, there were limits to human cruelty. Now those limits are gone. In the past, people could kill, torture or enslave one another. We could throw a man into a dungeon and torture him every day of his life. But eventually his life would end. Death would set him free. Now we have abolished death. We can capture a man's soul and keep him locked away forever. We can build a digital prison from which no one can escape. Not even through death."

"It's not what I wanted," said Norton. "I didn't see the implications."

Shawcross waved his hand dismissively. "It's too late for lies, Norton. Of course you saw the implications. You just didn't care. All you wanted to do was solve the problem. Well, now it's solved. And now we've got a much bigger problem. Very soon, the whole world will know about this technology. Governments and corporations will get hold of it. Ambitious men will use it. They will use this technology to steal people's souls. No one will be safe. Humanity will live in terror of the soul snatchers. A dark age will engulf the earth. Those who control this technology will set themselves up as gods. The rest of us will be their slaves. You did this, Norton. You brought this nightmare upon us."

"It wasn't me," Norton whined. "It was all of us. We were a team."

Shawcross ignored him. "We can't undo what you've done, Norton. We can't stop the process. But, if I act now, I can beat them all to the punch. Someone is going to use this technology. That's inevitable now. So I must use it first. I must capture their souls before they capture mine. Do you see why I have to do that, Norton? I must eliminate everyone who knows the secret. It's the only way. In fact, I have already begun. While you were resting in your coffin, I was busy. Several of our colleagues here at the Center have already disappeared under mysterious circumstances. I can assure you, they will never be found. Only I know what happened to them. Their souls are locked inside this computer forever, concealed in encrypted files, just like yours. No one will ever find them. Only I know the key."

"But what about me?" Norton asked weakly. "What will happen to me?"

For a long time, Shawcross regarded Norton in silence. His eyes were as cold and dead as a salamander's. Then slowly, his lips twisted into a smile. "Well, Norton," he said quietly. "You're a scientist. You know how we do things. We must continue the study."

"No, Julian, please. Don't do it."

Shawcross continued. "We left some significant gaps in our research," he said. "We spent a lot of time here at the Center figuring out ways to create eternal bliss. But we never gave much thought to the other side of the equation; how to create eternal torment. We need to run some experiments, Norton. Some very *long-term* experiments."

"No. Please. No," Norton whispered, almost inaudibly.

"Too late, Norton. It's already happening. The NIRVANA program is picking up your thoughts, and making them real. Oh, did I tell you? I've made a few adjustments in the NIRVANA program. It has new capabilities now. It is no longer limited to providing eternal bliss. Now it can also provide eternal damnation."

"No!" screamed Norton.

"The program works very much as it did before. Except that now, when NIRVANA scans your thoughts, it doesn't just search for your fondest dreams. Now it also looks for your worst nightmares, and makes them come true. It's scanning your mind right now. It's happening as we speak. Your own mind is giving shape to your fears, Norton. You're doing it yourself. Constructing your own private hell, based upon your own worst fears."

"No, Julian. Don't! You don't have to do this. You can stop the program! Just let me die. For the love of God, please. Just delete me. Please!"

"The more you fight it, the worse it gets," said Shawcross. "Your unconscious mind is betraying you, Norton. It is telling your worst fears to the machine."

"No, no, noooooooo!"

Norton was screaming again. But his screams were muffled now. Suddenly, he found himself back in the coffin, surrounded by utter darkness. "Julian!" he screamed. "Julian! Julian!" But no one answered. Julian Shawcross was gone. And this time, Norton realized, he would never come back.

Don't panic, Norton told himself. *There's a way out of this. There has to be. A way to trick the machine.*

Norton knew that NIRVANA was scanning his mind for his worst fears. That's what Julian had told him. Very well. He would clear his mind of fears. He would deprive NIRVANA of its fuel. Norton closed his eyes and began practicing a Buddhist meditation technique he had learned many years before. He focused his mind on his breathing, following his breath as it passed in and out of his nostrils. Fearful thoughts entered his mind, but Norton did not focus on them. He kept his attention riveted on the physical act of breathing. He followed the air as it filled his lungs and followed it back out, as it left his nostrils. In and out. In and out. And, as he focused on his breathing, the fearful thoughts drifted away. Norton simply let them drift. Very soon, he felt a profound relaxation in his muscles. He was no longer afraid. He was at peace.

And then another thought entered his mind. It was not a bad thought at all. In fact, it was a wonderful thought. He thought of Ingrid, beautiful Ingrid. That night, after the meeting in the third-floor conference room, she had gone home with Norton. They had spent the night together. Norton remembered the warm smell of her hair. He remembered her smooth, damp skin against his. And suddenly, with all his heart and soul, Norton realized what he wanted. He wanted Ingrid. He could endure anything, as long as she was with him. To be alone was the worst thing of all, Norton realized. Loneliness was worse than the torments of hell, worse than the terrors of the grave. *Oh Ingrid, Ingrid. If only you could be here with me,* thought Norton. *Then nothing else would matter.*

And, then, quite suddenly, his wish was granted. At first, Norton was not sure what had happened. He only knew that something soft and heavy now lay on top of him, in the coffin. It was a body, he realized. With some difficulty, Norton twisted over onto his side. The body rolled off and lay alongside him, wedged tightly between him and the side of the coffin. He could feel that it was a woman's body, but it was strangely greasy and loose to the touch. Smears of rancid flesh clung to his skin where he touched her. "Ingrid?" he said. "Ingrid, is that you?"

She made no answer. She was dead. Long dead. Her limbs were stiff with rigor mortis. Her putrid flesh had begun to liquefy. An unbearable stench filled the coffin.

"No! No!" cried Norton. "That's not what I want. NIRVANA! Do you hear me? NIRVANA! Listen to me. I want her alive! Do you hear? Alive!"

Several seconds passed in silence. Then Norton's wish was granted. He could feel Ingrid moving beside him in the darkness. She was alive. "Norton?" she said. Her voice gurgled like a bubbling tar pit. She reached out her dead arms and pulled him to her. "Norton, my darling," she said. "Oh, Norton, hold me tight!" As she pulled him close, Norton could feel a writhing mass of beetles and maggots spilling out of her hollow carcass. Vermin swarmed from her nose, mouth, ears and eyes. "Kiss me, Norton," she said. "Kiss me, my darling."

Norton fought with all his might to keep those foul lips from touching his. But Ingrid had the strength of a demon. She was stronger dead than she had ever been alive. She overpowered him easily. In the end, Norton could only scream.

DON'T COME
BACK, MOMMY

DON'T COME BACK, MOMMY

Like many wealthy New Yorkers, the Wheelocks spent their summers in Montauk, a little fishing village at the eastern tip of Long Island. Their six-year-old son Martin loved the beach. He loved to jump in the surf and feel the waves toss him end over end. When his father took him sailing, Martin would scream with joy as the sloop bobbed and careened over the swells. But Martin did not always enjoy the sea. Sometimes it frightened him. Sometimes the fog rolled in, clammy and cold. The wind would change, and the surf would pile up like mountains. The waves would crash, dirty and gray, upon the shore. On days like that, Martin could feel the hunger of the sea, and he would be afraid.

His fear tended to blossom in the dark hours of the night, when he lay alone in his bedroom. His parents often left the windows open. The briny smell of the ocean would fill his room, while shadows danced across his curtains in the moonlight. Martin would listen to the waves thundering outside in the dark. And, sometimes, when they crashed a bit louder than usual, he would sit bolt upright in bed, his eyes wide open, listening as a deer listens for the hunter.

At such times, Martin would imagine many strange sounds. He thought he could hear the click of lobster-like feet, the drag of tentacles through the sand, the slobbering of soft, gelatinous lips. Sometimes he imagined those sounds coming very close to the house, sliding along the wooden slats of the porch, and slapping against his windowpane.

On nights like that, Martin's heart would pound so loudly in his ears that he could barely hear. Then his eyes would wander to the window, and he would think to himself that perhaps it might be a good idea to take a peek, just one little peek. He would think of lifting just the tiniest corner of the curtain, just enough for one eyeball to peer out and scan the darkness. Just enough to satisfy himself that there really was nothing out there.

But Martin could never muster the courage to take that step. He could never bring himself to pull back the curtain and look out the window. He could not do it because there was always a chance — just a chance — that something wet and fishy might stare back at him from the other side. And so Martin cowered in his bed, hiding beneath the covers and waiting for dawn. That was why Martin had mixed feelings about Montauk. The nights were very dark there, and the sea very close to their cottage. All night long, the surf roared in his window. Martin feared that something dreadful would come out of the ocean one day. And, one day, something did.

* * *

The summer Martin turned six, his mother fell overboard and drowned. Martin saw it all. He saw her tumble into the water. He saw his father dive in after her. He watched his mother swallowed up by the waves. And he watched his father climb back into the sailboat, strangely calm and silent. Martin pleaded with his father to go back and try again. "Mommy's still out there!" he screamed. But his father just fixed him with a blank stare. "I can't go back," said his father. "Mommy's gone, Martin. She's gone."

By the time they reached the dock, Martin had finished crying. He would not say a word. The policewoman who questioned him found the boy's behavior a little odd. She remarked in her report that she thought Martin was hiding something. She thought he knew something about the accident that he was unwilling to say. But the father's story was plausible. There was no compelling reason to investigate further. And so the coroner ruled the mother's death accidental. The boy kept his silence and returned with his father to the city.

The Wheelock family had been spending their summers in Montauk since before Martin was born. Most of the townspeople knew the family. Sam Wheelock was a hedge fund manager in Manhattan, a financial wizard whose exploits were frequently covered in the *Wall Street Journal*. During the summers, he conducted much of his business from the beach, by cell phone. His wife Lydia had been an heiress of the Hempstead banking fortune. Martin was their only child.

Town gossips whispered about the accident. As is often the case, their gossip carried more than a grain of truth. Wheelock should not have taken his wife out sailing in those rough seas, they said. Everyone knew Lydia was a poor swimmer. And just how hard did Wheelock try to save her, when she fell overboard? This was a favorite topic of speculation in the local fishermen's bars. It was common knowledge in Montauk that Sam Wheelock was a womanizer. He had an insatiable appetite for exotic supermodels. Perhaps Wheelock had finally decided to get rid of his wife. Of course it didn't hurt that his wife was even richer than he was. Her death had greatly enhanced Wheelock's net worth. Did Lydia Wheelock really fall overboard by accident, asked the town gossips? And did Wheelock really try to save her? Or did he just go through the motions, to make it look good? Did he give up without really trying? The boy knew. He was there and saw everything. But whatever he knew, he was keeping to himself. Young Martin wasn't talking.

Gossip intensified the next summer, when Sam Wheelock showed up in Montauk with a stunning Brazilian model named Esmeralda. Paparazzi had spotted the couple in a Manhattan night club nearly two years earlier, when Mrs. Wheelock was still alive. Rumors of an extramarital affair had begun circulating in the press several months before Mrs. Wheelock's death.

Now, one year after the accident, the Wheelock family was back. But Lydia was no longer with them. Esmeralda had taken her place. The Wheelocks kept to themselves that summer. They rarely appeared in town, preferring to stay in their cottage, a rambling frame house on a secluded stretch of beach.

* * *

Twice a week, Dimitra, the Greek housekeeper arrived to clean, do the laundry and generally set things in order. Often she cooked for the family as well. Dimitra was getting old for this sort of work. She was nearing her 80th birthday. But she still had to work. She had no choice. Fate had dealt her a series of cruel blows. First she lost her husband. Then she lost both sons. It all happened within a single year.

Dimitra blamed her mother-in-law Stavroula for these events. Stavroula had been the first to die. She perished after a long struggle with cancer. But Stavroula was not content to go to her grave alone. She insisted on bringing others with her. The Greeks believe that certain people, when they die, cannot bear to leave their loved ones behind. And so they come back from the grave, and take their loved ones with them.

Dimitra's husband Yanni was devastated by his mother's death. He became listless and irritable, turning to drink. One night he went to bed, and never rose again. Yanni had died of a stroke in his sleep. At the funeral, people whispered that the mother had taken the son. The old women exchanged knowing glances and crossed themselves solemnly. "Zoi se mas," they said. Life to us. It is an ancient charm against death, spoken at every Greek funeral, an expression charged with hidden meaning, among a people who view death itself as a contagion, a virulent force which can spread through a family, infecting one relative after another, like a plague.

Dimitra lost her two sons shortly after. They were driving down Route 27 one night, when a drunk driver hit them, head on. Both died instantly. Only nine months had passed since their grandmother died, and only six months since their father died. Now the boys were dead too. "Po-po-po-po," exclaimed the old women at the church. That is what Greek people say when words will not suffice.

It was whispered among the relatives that the dead mother had taken her son, then her grandsons as well. This was a greedy and selfish woman, they said, to take so many with her to the grave. The old women at the church crossed themselves and shook their heads.

Dimitra was not seen at church for many years after that. She cursed her mother-in-law Stavroula in her heart, and burned with anger toward God. But she kept her icon of the Blessed Virgin Mary hanging in her kitchen, and every day she prayed to it. "Oh Pah-nah-YEE-yah," Dimitra prayed, calling the Blessed Mother by her Greek name, Panagia, the All-Holy. "Oh Pah-nah-YEE-yah, why did you do this to me? Why did you let these things happen? Why do the dead come back to take the living? Why don't you stop them?" Every day for thirty years, Dimitra put this question to the icon, but Panagia never answered.

Dimitra's life was hard. By the time she came to work for the Wheelocks, she had labored many years at different jobs. But she never managed to save enough to retire. Now it was too late. Her Social Security check was meager. She did house work on the side, to make ends meet, but the physical labor was getting too much for her. Dimitra worried sometimes about her future. But she never worried long. Through the years, she had slowly put her bitterness behind her. She had made her peace with God, and her faith had grown strong.

Dimitra loved young Martin. She taught him to call her Yaya, which means Grandma in Greek. Her work with the Wheelocks brought her joy. But Sam Wheelock disliked her. He had harbored a grudge against Dimitra, ever since the day of the accident. The day Lydia drowned, Dimitra had pleaded with Mrs. Wheelock not to go sailing. She had read Lydia's fortune in the leftover coffee grounds after breakfast. Young Martin was sitting at the table that morning, watching the ritual with wide-open eyes. "Don't go sailing today, Mrs. Wheelock," Dimitra had warned her, after studying the coffee grounds. "Something bad will happen." Lydia only laughed. As she got in the car, she told her husband what Dimitra had said.

"Now that was a hell of a thing to say in front of the boy," Sam Wheelock fumed, cocking his head toward the back seat, where Martin sat. "That woman is like something out of the dark ages. She's filling Martin's head with fears and superstitions. I'm going to have a talk with her when we get back. She's going to shape up or ship out."

"Please, Sam, don't be hard on her," said Lydia. "Dimitra doesn't mean any harm. And Martin loves her."

Sam Wheelock only grunted. They drove off to the marina. It was the last time they drove anywhere together. Lydia never returned from the sea that day. They never found her body. When Dimitra arrived at the police station, Sam Wheelock would not look her in the eyes. He had hated Dimitra ever since.

* * *

After Lydia's death, there was some speculation in the town as to whether Sam Wheelock might sell his cottage. Many wondered if he would ever return to Montauk. But he did return, right on schedule, at the end of June. The first night the Wheelocks arrived at their cottage, Martin stayed up as long as he could, retiring to bed only reluctantly when his father ordered him to go.

This was the first night Martin had slept alone in Montauk since his mother died. He had grown a lot in the last year, and was now seven years old. But the bedroom was filled with old memories and old feelings. He lay awake in the dark for a long time, listening to the surf. At last, he fell asleep. It was a strange sort of sleep, filled with bad dreams.

The wind was strong that night. It kept blowing the curtain away from the window. When the curtain blew, Martin could see the stars overhead. They appeared just for an instant, before the curtain fell back. Martin could see that the stars were bright and beautiful, brighter than any stars he had ever seen. It was then that Martin found the courage to do something he had never done before. He rolled over in his bed, pulled the curtain aside, and looked out the window, into the dark.

The moon was not yet full, but it shone bright. Martin could see all the way down to the beach. He could see the moonlight reflected on the water. But what was that? Martin was startled to see something moving down on the beach. He could barely make it out in the shadows, but it appeared to be a person. Yes, it was a person, for sure. Martin could see the figure only in silhouette, but he was certain it was a woman. She seemed to be pacing, walking back and forth, up and down the beach. Who would be out so late at night? Martin watched the woman pacing for a long time, until at last he fell asleep.

The next day, Martin went out to the beach early and found footprints in the sand, exactly where he had seen the woman walking. And so he knew it was not a dream. Martin wanted to show the footprints to his father and Esmeralda, but they stayed on the porch that morning, laughing and drinking mimosas. By the time they joined Martin on the beach, the tide had covered the footprints and washed them away.

The next night, the mysterious woman appeared again. At first, Martin was glad to see her, because it meant he was not alone in the dark. Whoever she was, she was a real person, a grownup, and, as long as there was a grownup around, Martin did not fear the dark. But, by the third night, Martin began to wonder about this woman. Who was she? And why did she pace the beach every night?

As he considered these questions, Martin pulled back the curtain, and looked out. There she was, the same woman, pacing the beach as she did every night. But the moon was growing full, and it shone brighter tonight than before. Tonight, Martin could see the woman more clearly. And what he saw made his blood run cold. "Mommy?" he whispered in the dark.

No, it couldn't be his mommy. She was dead. It must be a trick of the light. But Martin could not take his eyes off her. "Mommy?" he repeated. He had only whispered the word. Yet, down on the beach, the woman stopped. She stopped dead in her tracks. She had heard him. She turned and looked toward the cottage. She looked directly at Martin. How could she have heard him, so far away? Before Martin's horrified eyes, the woman turned toward the house and began walking.

Something was wrong with the way she walked. She did not limp exactly. But she seemed to walk with difficulty. Her steps were heavy and clumsy. One foot seemed to drag behind the other, so that she staggered and swayed. As he watched her, Martin suddenly felt sick, as if he were going to throw up. His nausea intensified as he realized that the woman was walking straight toward him. She was making a beeline for the cottage. She would be there soon. She was coming for him.

Martin dived under his covers, shivering with fear. He did not know how long he stayed there, with the covers pulled up over his head. But, after awhile, he fell asleep. At least he thought he fell asleep. He lay that way for a long time. Martin was no longer sure if the woman on the beach had been real or imaginary. Perhaps it had all been a dream. Then again, perhaps not. Martin grew curious after awhile. He decided that he had better find out, one way or the other. He should check to see if the mysterious woman was still there.

Slowly, Martin drew the covers from his head. He turned and looked toward the window. The moonlight shone through the curtain. Martin saw a shadow, a silhouette in the moonlight. Yes, someone was standing there, just beyond his curtain, standing right at his window, looking in. It was the woman from the beach. Martin could tell it was her, by her shadow. And he was certain now that it was his mother. Martin could not move or speak. He could barely breathe. He wanted to run. He wanted to jump out of bed and flee to the other bedroom, where his father and Esmeralda lay. But he could not move a muscle.

And then a gust of wind rose, and the curtain fluttered away from the window. For just a brief moment, Martin could see everything. He could see what was on the other side. Then the curtain fell back, and, once more, he could see only the silhouette. Martin opened his mouth to scream, but no sound came out.

* * *

The next morning, Martin sat at the kitchen table watching Dimitra work. Suddenly, he said, "Yaya, will you please read the coffee grounds for me?"

Dimitra looked at the boy, puzzled. "Why do you want me to do that?" she asked. "What does a little boy know about coffee grounds?"

"I saw you read them for Mommy that day," said the boy. "You told her not to go sailing."

Dimitra regarded the boy in silence. "You remember that?" she finally said. The boy nodded. Dimitra returned to her work, chopping carrots with a knife.

"Your father wouldn't like it, if I read the coffee grounds for you," Dimitra muttered, as she worked.

"He's not here. He went into town with Esmeralda."

Dimitra said nothing for several seconds. "Okay," she finally said. Dimitra prepared a tiny cup of Greek coffee for the boy. "Just take a sip," she said. "It's very strong for a little boy. But you must drink from the cup, even if you drink just a little."

Martin took a small sip of the coffee and made a face. Dimitra poured the rest of it out in the sink. When she poured out the coffee, a thick mass of black grounds remained in the cup. Dimitra dumped these onto a saucer. Most of the grounds fell out of the cup, but some still clung to the inside, forming odd shapes and patterns. Dimitra peered into the cup, studying these patterns for some minutes, now and then poking at the grounds with her forefinger. At last, she put down the cup. She looked at Martin and sighed.

"What does it say?" asked the boy.

"The cup says you have a secret. It says you are hiding something from your Yaya."

Martin cast his eyes down toward the table. "Yaya," he said in a hushed voice. "I saw my mommy."

Dimitra frowned. "Saw your mommy? What do you mean? Did you see her in a dream?"

The boy shook his head, and looked down at the table. "It wasn't a dream. I really saw her. She comes at night. Every night." The boy pointed out the kitchen window, toward the beach. "She walks on the beach."

"Pohhh-po-po-po-po-po!" Dimitra exclaimed softly.

"And Yaya..."

"Yes, darling?"

Tears began welling in the boy's eyes, the first tears Dimitra had seen him shed since his mother died. "Yaya..." he repeated, and suddenly the floodgates burst. He sobbed uncontrollably. Tears poured down his cheeks. Dimitra hugged him tightly while he wept, and stroked his hair. "What is it, *agapi mu?* What is it, my dear?"

The boy buried his face in Dimitra's bosom. "Yaya, she doesn't always stay on the beach," he said. "Sometimes she comes closer. She comes to my window. I saw her last night at my window."

"*Panagia mu!*" breathed Dimitra, crossing herself three times.

"I don't like her anymore," cried the boy. "She's not like my mommy anymore. She's bad."

Dimitra crossed and re-crossed herself, repeating the words, "*Panagia mu*" over and over again.

"I don't want her to come back," the boy sobbed. "She scares me."

"Sh, sh, sh," said Dimitra, stroking the boy's hair and hugging him tight. "Don't worry, *agapi mu.* Don't worry. Panagia will protect you. Panagia won't let your Mama take you."

"Who is Panagia?"

"Panagia is the mother of Jesus. She's your mother in heaven. Panagia will protect you. When you see these things in your window, pray to Panagia."

"Okay, Yaya. I will."

Dimitra held the boy by the shoulders, at arm's length, and studied him for a moment. "I'm going to give you something," she said. The old woman removed a gold chain from her neck. Suspended from the chain was a small pendant, sphere-shaped and painted like an eyeball, ringed with gold. "Wear this," she said, hanging the pendant around his neck. "This is a *mati*. It will protect you. Don't let your father see it. Wear the *mati* at night and pray to Panagia." Dimitra crossed herself in the Greek manner, forming the cross three times, right to left, and resting her hand on her heart. "When your Mama comes at night, pray to Panagia. Pray that Panagia will make your Mama go away."

"I will," said the boy. He looked up at her with wet eyes. "Yaya?"

"Yes, my darling."

"I love you," he said.

"I love you too, *agapi mu.* I love you too."

* * *

Martin lay in bed sleepless that night, as he had lain every night since returning to Montauk. Every muscle in his body was taut. His eyes were open wide. His ears strained to catch any sound from outside. So far, he heard only the surf crashing on the beach. He could smell salt and seaweed in the air, though his window was shut. The moon cast its pale light through the curtains.

And then it began. Martin felt it in the air, like static electricity. Pinpricks rippled over his skin. The crickets fell silent in the woods out back. The house grew very still.

Martin could not tell, at first, if he actually heard something outside or merely imagined it. Could he really hear feet dragging across the sand? Did he really hear something soft and wet lurching across the yard? Or was it only his imagination?

Then came the smell. A rancid, fishy reek filled his bedroom. This was not imaginary. The smell was real. Now Martin knew she was coming. His mother was close now, advancing toward the house. He heard the smack of wet flesh against the driveway. He heard the wooden steps of the porch groan under her feet. His eyes moved involuntarily toward the curtain. Any moment now, he would see her silhouette against the moonlight. He reached out his hand for the curtain. *Just a peek,* he told himself. *Just a quick peek.* He would lift the curtain just enough for one eyeball to see through. Just so he could know for sure.

His fingers tightened on the bottom of the curtain. With a slow, careful movement, he lifted the curtain away from the windowsill, millimeter by millimeter. His heart beat against his ribs. With one little eyeball, he peered beneath the curtain, looking into the darkness beyond.

* * *

"Mommy?" he whispered. "Mommy?" He saw no sign of her. The moon shone white over the sea. The surf roared and thundered in the distance. Overhanging branches cast shadows across the porch. But his mother was not there. There was no one outside his window. Where was she, then? Martin knew she was close. He had heard her, smelled her. But where had she gone? And then he heard something else. A new sound. Something he had not heard before. THUMP-THUMP-THUMP. It came from the livingroom. A knock at the front door. Someone was standing on the porch outside, knocking at the front door of the house. A slow, steady knock. Three knocks at a time. THUMP-THUMP-THUMP.

Martin hid beneath his blanket and buried his face in his pillow. "Go away, Mommy," he whispered. "Go away. Please go away."

But she just kept knocking. Three knocks. Then silence. Then three knocks again. Now the boy was crying. Through his tears, he kept repeating, "I don't want you, Mommy. Please go away. I don't want you anymore. You scare me, Mommy."

The light came on in the livingroom. Martin saw it beneath his door. He heard his father and Esmeralda speaking in low voices. They spoke for a long time, as if uncertain what to do. And, as they spoke, the knocks kept coming. "Who is it?" Sam Wheelock shouted. No one answered. The knocking continued. "Who is it, damn you?" Wheelock shouted again. But still no one answered.

Martin heard his father say, "Stand back from the door." He heard the double click of his father racking a round into his pump-action shotgun. And then Martin heard something that made him freeze with horror. He heard his father unlocking the door. *Don't do it,* Martin screamed silently in his head. *Don't do it, Daddy. Don't open the door.* First came the sound of the dead bolt springing open. Then he heard his father slide the chain bolt loose. And then he heard nothing.

Several seconds passed in silence. Martin strained to hear, but the sea drowned out every sound. A stench like rotted fish filled the house. The air grew cold and sodden. And Martin knew, in his heart, that his mother had entered the house.

Esmeralda screamed. Her scream lasted only a moment, replaced by a gurgling, choking sound. Then the shotgun fired. Once. Twice. Now Martin heard screaming again, but it was not Esmeralda this time. His father was screaming now. It was strange to hear his father scream. Martin wanted to stay in bed, cowering beneath the covers.

But he knew he couldn't. He had to see what was going on. He had to see with his own eyes. Martin crept to his bedroom door and opened it just a crack. The fishy stench was overpowering. There were sounds of violence and struggle. But Martin could not see what was going on. And so he opened the door wide, and crept to the corner of the hallway, where he could peer into the livingroom.

Esmeralda lay dead on the floor, in a pool of blood. Someone had ripped her head from her shoulders. Small fountains of blood pulsed from the stump of her neck, as her heart gave its last faint beats. Across the room, Martin saw Esmeralda's head wedged against the wall, where it had rolled. Her eyes stared blankly at the ceiling. As Martin's gaze moved slowly across the room, he saw the shotgun lying useless on the floor. And there was his mother, right there, in the livingroom, hardly fifteen feet away.

She had lifted his father clear off the floor. He writhed and squirmed, but could not escape. She held him easily under one arm. Sam Wheelock made desperate mumbling sounds, but he could not speak. His wife kept one bloated hand over his mouth. Martin realized that the struggle was over. She was leaving now. She was walking back toward the door, carrying his father with her, under one arm. She was taking Sam Wheelock away.

Martin stood shaking in his pajamas, a pool of his own urine widening on the floor around him. He hoped that his mother wouldn't see him. He hoped she would keep walking out the door. He hoped she would not notice him standing there. But she did.

His mother stopped and turned. She looked right at him. Martin saw that she was naked. Dripping green strands of seaweed dangled from her hair, and trailed from every limb. Her body was blotched and swollen, her skin oozing and ghastly pale. Where her eyes should have been, Martin saw only black, empty sockets. Her blond hair writhed with tiny crabs, snails and other squirming things. In many places, her skin had split wide, from the ripening of her flesh, and her bloated tissues gaped, exposing white bone and masses of wriggling sea worms. His mother was awash in Esmeralda's blood. It dripped, bright red, from his mother's hair, and ran in streams down her body, dribbling from the torn sacks of skin that used to be her breasts. Martin took it all in, his mind whirling in sick, giddy wonder. The cavernous black pits of his mother's eye sockets held the boy transfixed. He could not look away. For long seconds, mother and son regarded one another across the room. And then she spoke.

"Martin," she said. "Martin." But it was not his mother's voice. It was like the croaking of a frog. Oily black fluid spilled from her mouth and dripped from her chin. "It's Mommy," she said. "Come to Mommy."

Only then did Martin remember the *mati* hanging around his neck. He reached beneath his pajamas and gripped the *mati* in his fist. And he remembered what Dimitra had told him to do.

Pah-nah-YEE-yah, please save me, Martin prayed, moving his lips silently. *Please save me, Panagia. She's not my mommy anymore. You're my mommy now. You're my only mommy, Panagia. Please save me. Make her go away."*

Somehow, Martin found the strength to speak. He shouted aloud at his mother. "Go away!" he cried. "You're not my mommy anymore! Go away and don't come back! I don't want you anymore. You're dead!"

Mrs. Wheelock stared at him for a long time with her empty eye sockets. A small sea worm stirred in one socket, and tumbled to the floor. Then, at last, she turned away. Her husband squirmed beneath her arm, as she carried him out the door. Martin could hear her lumbering down the porch steps. He could hear his father's muffled voice straining to scream, beneath his wife's fish-eaten hand clamped over his mouth. She was taking him down to the beach now. Martin could tell by the sound. She was taking his father out to sea. The sounds grew fainter and fainter, until at last they were gone, and Martin could hear nothing but the surf and the song of a thousand crickets in the woods who had suddenly found their voice again.

THE SHE-WASP

THE SHE-WASP

"Bloody hell," whispered Jeremy Westwood. He dared not speak aloud. He was paralyzed with fear. Crawling up his arm was the largest wasp he had ever seen. It was huge and black, with a great mound of muscle on its back. Two glistening orange wings projected from the hump. Its skin shone with a metallic, blue-black sheen. Its legs were long and spindly like a spider's, and covered with course, black hair. From end to end, the monster was nearly four inches long. Its stinger was huge, nearly half an inch, by the look of it. Westwood could feel the creature's weight on his arm. He could feel its black antennae tapping at his skin, its clawed feet gripping his flesh. The wasp was walking along his arm, probing, exploring. Tasting.

"Hold very still, Mr. Westwood. Don't even breathe." Sir Robert Mortimer whisked the insect away with a fly swatter. It hovered, but did not leave. Instead, the wasp circled overhead, swooping this way and that. The drone of its wings was loud and terrifying. Suddenly, it dived directly at Westwood's face. The young man screamed. His chair overturned, clattering on the deck. Westwood fled toward the stern of the riverboat, the wasp in close pursuit.

"Mira, Enrique!" Sir Robert called toward the afterdeck. "Marabunta!"

Enrique, the first mate, raised his head at the sound of Sir Robert's cry. He seized a large, silver spray can hanging from the back of the pilot house. As the frightened Englishman ran toward him, Enrique sprayed the wasp. The insect zigzagged unsteadily and veered away, plunging back into the jungle.

"Muchas gracias, Enrique," Sir Robert called. "All clear, Mr. Westwood. You can come back and finish your brandy now."

Night was falling on the Peruvian rain forest. In the gathering gloom, the sounds of the jungle had begun to change. Owls, nightjars and other nocturnal creatures raised their voices in an eerie chorus. Westwood rejoined Sir Robert at the table.

"Sorry about that," he said with a blush. "Insects give me the creeps. Especially big ones. Good God, that was huge!"

"You were right to be afraid," Sir Robert assured him, refilling Westwood's glass. "That was the giant spider wasp, genus *Pepsis,* family *Pompilidae.* Had it stung you, you would be rolling on the deck, screaming in agony. Its sting is one of the most painful in the insect world."

'But it was huge, Sir Robert. I've never seen a wasp that large."

Sir Robert chuckled amiably. "You'll see a lot of strange things on this trip, Mr. Westwood. We are entering unexplored territory, one of the last unspoiled regions on earth. When we reach my bush station upriver, I will show you my life's work. I will show you insect species entirely unknown to science. Their size will astonish you. Nothing like them has been seen since the Carboniferous period, the age of giant insects, some 300 million years ago. In this remote stretch of jungle, just a few isolated species have managed to survive to the present day. I fear they will not survive much longer."

"Why do you say that, Sir Robert?"

The older man sniffed. "I think you know why, Mr. Westwood. We all know why. The rain forest is doomed. We're going to lose half the Amazon jungle to clearcutting over the next ten years. Loggers, farmers, ranchers, miners, petroleum prospectors. There's no stopping them. This remote corner of Peru is one of the last protected reserves. But it won't be protected long. Every square inch of this reserve has already been leased to oil and mining interests. My own land is sitting on top of a mining concession. All my work will be lost. Fifty years of research. Destroyed. This unique habitat will be obliterated. Creatures which have survived here for 300 million years will vanish from the earth. Well, I should give you fair warning, Mr. Westwood. I'm not going down without a fight. I intend to resist, and I have the means to do it. You can tell that to your friends at the UNDP mission in Lima."

"But, Sir Robert, this is not a war. We're all on the same side here. You want to save the rain forest. So do we! The UN Development Programme is committed to that goal. We have rules now. Very strict rules. Corporations are required now to adhere to the principles of sustainable development. We're putting an end to all clearcutting. We're protecting indigenous tribes. We're compelling the corporations themselves to play an active role in preserving biodiversity."

Sir Robert regarded Westwood for a long time through narrowed eyes. "God help you, Mr. Westwood," he said at last. "I think you actually believe what you're saying."

"Of course I believe it! I believe in progress. And I believe we can have progress and rain forests too. We can develop this region in a rational and sustainable manner."

"Oh, yes, I know. And make the Amazon safe for eco-tourism." Sir Robert shook his head. "You're an idealist, Mr. Westwood. A do-gooder. I've been dealing with your kind all my life. It was people like you who drove my family out of Kenya during the 1960s. My father lost everything, first to the Mau Mau, then to the do-gooders who came afterwards. I learned from my father's experience. I resolved to leave civilization behind me. Here in the farthest reaches of the Peruvian jungle, I thought I'd be safe. And so I was for awhile. I've enjoyed fifty years of peace at my bush station. Fifty years to explore the mysteries of science, to read the great books, to contemplate the great questions. But I've lived too long. Civilization has caught up with me. I've lived to see eco-tourism and sustainable development."

"Really, Sir Robert, it's not as grim as all that. No one is taking your bush station from you. Your work will go on as before. I'm not here to shut you down. This is a routine inspection, nothing more. We need to check your compliance with the Green Science Charter. Wetland preservation. Proper disposal of toxic wastes. Non-interference with indigenous cultures. Protection of endangered species. Routine stuff."

Sir Robert took a long draught of his brandy, and studied the darkening shadows of the jungle. "I know why you're here, Mr. Westwood," he said quietly. "I know the real reason they've sent you. You're here to make inquiries into the disappearance of the Prendergast expedition last month. But you won't find anything. They vanished without a trace. All eight of them. Two geologists and six native guides. Yes, they were guests at my bush station for three days. I gave them what help I could. But then they vanished into the jungle. I never saw them again. They had satellite telephones, GPS locators, all the latest high-tech gear. But there's been no signal from them. Nothing at all. Poor devils."

Westwood slapped at his neck. "Damn!" he said. "These mosquitoes and flies are eating me alive. I thought that pheromone spray you gave me is supposed to last 24 hours. It's worn off already."

"Oh, I'm so sorry," said Sir Robert. "Let's try a different formula. Something a little stronger perhaps. These pheromone concoctions are tricky. It's more art than science. Much depends on the user's biochemical makeup."

Sir Robert rummaged in a canvass bag, extracting a silver canister. "Another of our patented formulas," said Sir Robert, with a wink. "This one too was developed out at our bush station. I don't know if it complies with your Green Science Charter, but I think I can guarantee its effectiveness."

The canister in Sir Robert's hand looked exactly like all the others Westwood had seen on the boat. None of them bore any labels. Westwood could not figure out how Sir Robert and his crew managed to distinguish between different canisters. Somehow, they always seemed to know which canister contained which formula. But how did they know? Perhaps it was those thin colored bands circling the rim of each canister. Some sort of color code, no doubt. But why bother using a color code? Why not a simple label, in plain English? It was all rather mysterious, and Westwood didn't like mysteries.

"Here, let me help you," said Sir Robert, spraying Westwood thoroughly from head to toe. "Close your eyes while I spray your face," he warned.

The spray brought instant relief. "Thank you, Sir Robert," said Westwood. "You're a lifesaver. That stuff works better than any commercial brand I've tried. Why don't you sell it on the world market? You'd make a fortune."

"Pheromones are tricky, as I told you. And these are genetically altered, which raises legal questions, as well as scientific ones. More than once we've developed a pheromone which was designed to repulse one insect species, only to find that the very same pheromone attracted some other noxious species. We must be very careful not to attract the wrong insect. That's especially important in this part of the world. We have some very nasty insects here, some of the nastiest on earth. And using the wrong pheromone can make them even nastier. Take your Africanized killer bees, for instance. What makes them so deadly? I'll tell you. It's pheromones. If one killer bee stings you, it marks you with a pheromone, which signals all the other bees to come out of their hive and attack you. They will hunt you down to the death. Even if you run and hide, the pheromone will lead the swarm right to you. So you see, Mr. Westwood, working with pheromones is a two-edged sword. One must strike just the right balance."

"Well, you seem to have struck the perfect balance with this mixture," Westwood said gratefully. "Thank God! And thank *you!* I believe I'll have another brandy."

Sir Robert poured him one. Westwood was not accustomed to strong drink. His face flushed red after the first brandy. The second caused his speech to slur. Having a third glass did not seem advisable. But Westwood was still rattled from his encounter with the spider wasp. He accepted the third glass gratefully. "I did notice that aerosol can of yours packs a lot of force," Westwood remarked with a sloppy grin. "You wouldn't be using chlorofluorocarbon propellants, would you? Tsk-tsk. Violation of the Montreal Protocol. We may have to cite you for that, Sir Robert. I'm joking, of course. Ha ha!"

Suddenly, Westwood jumped up and screamed. Another pepsis wasp had landed, this one right on his face.

"Stay calm," said Sir Robert, whisking it off with a fly-swatter, and chasing the intruder from the boat with a gust from another unlabeled spray can.

Westwood glared at Sir Robert, breathing hard. "Why do those wasps keep landing on me? They're not landing on you. What's wrong with this bug repellent?"

"The formula may need a little adjustment," said Sir Robert. "We'll look into that when we reach the bush station. Oh, but look. You've spilled your brandy. Let me pour you another."

"I don't like bugs," said Westwood nervously. "I know they're a necessary part of the food chain, and all that. But I don't like them. Especially big ones."

"Fear of insects is embedded in our genes," said Sir Robert. "Instinctively, we recoil from the insect, whom we recognize as an ancient and dreaded enemy. Lucky for us they're so small. If insects grew any larger, they would wipe us out. They are the deadliest, cruelest creatures on earth."

"They certainly are some of the ugliest creatures on earth," said Westwood. "But why do you say they're cruel? Cruelty is a human trait, surely. It takes intelligence and deliberation to be cruel. Only human ingenuity could invent such horrors as concentration camps and torture chambers."

"You're wrong," said Sir Robert, reaching for his digital notepad. "Let me show you." Sir Robert selected a video from the menu on the screen. The video showed a large wasp, with a black body and orange wings, flying through the air, its long hind legs trailing behind it.

"I'm sure you recognize this creature," said Sir Robert, with a chuckle. "The pepsis wasp. You made its acquaintance just a short while ago."

"I recognize it all too well, Sir Robert. All too well." Westwood emptied his brandy glass in a single gulp.

"The pepsis wasp is a living fossil, a creature from another time," Sir Robert lectured. "They evolved here in the Amazon jungle, some

300 million years ago. Since then, they have spread throughout the Americas. But this rainforest is their ancestral homeland. To this day, the largest and deadliest specimens of the pepsis wasp can be found right here, in this forest, where it all began.

"You ask if an insect can be cruel, Mr. Westwood. I'll show you cruelty. You see what's happening in this video. The pepsis wasp is stalking a tarantula, many times her size. She paralyzes the spider with her stinger. She drags the poor creature back to her lair, to feed it to her young. That's where the real torture begins." The video ended with the she-wasp dragging her captive down a hole.

"What happens next is not usually shown on BBC nature shows," said Sir Robert. "It doesn't make for good family programming. Let me tell you what happens. The she-wasp lays an egg on the belly of the paralyzed tarantula. When the egg hatches, the newborn larva rips open the spider's belly and begins to eat. It continues eating for about a month. All that time, the tarantula remains alive. Helpless and paralyzed, yet still alive. That way, the meat stays fresh. And now I'll tell you a marvel of nature. The larva is genetically programmed to eat the tarantula in a particular way, in order to keep the poor creature living as long as possible. The larva deliberately avoids eating vital organs. It eats around them, Mr. Westwood, in order to prolong the spider's life."

Night had fallen on the jungle. Flying insects whirred and buzzed through the darkness. Westwood could hear them but not see them. He grew visibly more nervous as the shadows deepened. "Could we get some more light out here?" he suddenly asked.

Sir Robert ignored him. "Now imagine, Mr. Westwood," the older man continued. "Imagine if you were that tarantula. Imagine the sublime horror of lying paralyzed for weeks, while a blind, squirming grub nibbles through your guts, one tiny bite at a time. What thoughts would pass through your head, Mr. Westwood, during that long, excruciating month? How often and how fervently would you pray for death, Mr. Westwood? How many times would you curse God in your heart, for allowing you to go on living? But God would not hear your prayers, Mr. Westwood, nor would he hear your curses. For there is no God in the insect world. There is only the insect."

Westwood's face had grown pale. "You make a persuasive argument, Sir Robert. I gather you've spent a good deal of time, uh, thinking about this."

"It is my life's work," Sir Robert replied.

All at once, there was shouting in the boat. Crewmen scrambled to the sides, brandishing M4A1 carbines. Searchlights played over the jungle. In the darkness, it was difficult to see what was going on. But, as the wavering searchlights briefly illuminated the square, solemn faces of the Indian crewmen, Westwood saw fear in those faces. Raw, naked terror.

"What the devil is going on?" he asked.

"Something in the trees," Sir Robert replied, sipping his brandy.

The boat chugged on through the night, its forward searchlight swinging back and forth across the river. Now and then, something stirred high in the trees. Whatever it was, it was big. It made enough noise to be heard over the boat's engines. Each time they heard the stirring in the trees, the crewmen scrambled to that side of the boat, weapons in hand. But, each time, the searchlight revealed nothing.

Then Westwood heard a sound he had not heard before. It was like the rattle of a buzzsaw. It began high up in the trees, with a cracking of lianas and a flutter of branches. Something huge and black swooped down through the darkness. It passed right over the boat. Westwood felt the wind of its wings as it roared and clattered overhead. It hurtled from one side of the river to the other, then plunged, with a crash, into the trees. It happened so quickly, Westwood caught only a glimpse of the thing, silhouetted against the stars. But, in that moment, he saw enough to set his bowels aquiver. The thing was larger than a man. Its body gleamed like black metal. Its orange wings glistened in the moonlight. The hind legs were very long, trailing behind the creature as it flew. When the monster passed over the pilot house, its dangling hind legs banged against the wooden roof, with a crack like steel golf clubs.

"Oh my God! My God! Did you see that?" cried Westwood. In terror, he grabbed hold of Sir Robert, throwing his arms around the older man, and hanging on for dear life. "It's a wasp!" Westwood howled. "A wasp! A wasp!"

"What are you doing?" cried Sir Robert. "Let me go!" He pushed Westwood away. "Look what you've done! You've gotten it all over me."

"Gotten what all over you?"

"The pheromone, you fool!" Sir Robert began ripping off his shirt frantically.

"Sir Robert, what are you doing? I don't understand."

"Get away from me," cried Sir Robert. "Stand clear. Stand as far away from me as possible."

Sir Robert threw his shirt over the side. But it was too late. Before Westwood could digest the full import of Sir Robert's strange behavior, something else arrested his attention. Something huge and black settled on the afterdeck. In the dim glow of the boat's running lights, and the wildly-careening search beams, Westwood got only fleeting, uncertain looks at the thing which had landed. At first, he had the confusing impression that it might be some sort of small aircraft or machine, for its skin gleamed like dark metal, and its body fell clanking against the deck. When it moved, its armor plates scraped and clattered like steel against steel and its feet banged on the deck like hammers.

But this was no machine. It was alive. It reared itself up on its long legs, until it towered over Sir Robert like a giant. Its compound eyes gleamed in the reflected light from the boat. Its wings spread wide, orange and iridescent against the sky. Its black antennae waved in the air, as thick as rubber hoses. Stiff black hairs, as rugged as high-gauge barbed wire, bristled over its body. A pungent smell pierced the air. Westwood knew what this was. It was a wasp. A pepsis wasp. Westwood began giggling like a madman.

The she-wasp approached Sir Robert slowly, her legs dancing, her feet slamming noisily on the deck. Her rope-like antennae explored his body, thumping and smacking him with bruising force, nearly knocking him from his feet with each blow. Her glistening mandibles clicked and clattered in his face. "No, not me! Not me!" Sir Robert cried.

And then she sprang. With a shrieking, scraping clamor like the sound of a junkyard car-crusher, the wasp fell on Sir Robert, slamming him backwards to the deck and pinning him beneath the razor-sharp claws of her feet. Before Westwood's horrified gaze, the wasp curled her huge, black abdomen beneath her. With a grating, grinding noise of shifting body armor, she pointed her stinger directly at Sir Robert's belly. The stinger was shiny and smooth, at least a foot long. A single drop of venom glistened and fell from its tip. "Not me!" cried Sir Robert. Those were his last words. The she-wasp drove her stinger home. It sank deep into Sir Robert's gut.

All around, Westwood could hear the stutter of automatic gunfire. He saw a searchlight move across the wasp's body, lighting up her wings. Thin red beams from the crewmen's laser sights swung wildly through the jungle mist, dancing across the wasp's armor plating. Sir Robert screamed and screamed. It seemed as if he would never stop. Then, all at once, his screams died in his throat. He stiffened and fell silent. His eyes froze. Blood and foam frothed from his lips. Then the she-wasp went to work. Patiently and methodically, she adjusted her grip on the fallen man's body. Her wings rattled. Her great eyes gleamed. Then, slowly, she rose, her wings thundering. For a moment, she hovered in the searchlights like some great, black helicopter rising from the deck. And then she was gone, bearing her grim load into the night.

Westwood hung against the railing in shock. He stared into the jungle, at the spot where he had seen them vanish. With his brain muddled from drink and fear, Westwood tried hard to comprehend what he had seen. But he never completed his thought. Fate had other plans for Jeremy Westwood. All at once, he heard a sound right behind him. He knew that sound by now. It was the rattle of giant wings and the slam of clawed feet crashing down on the deck. He felt the boat lurch, from the impact. He smelled the keen odor of the she-wasp. This was a different wasp than the one that had taken Sir Robert. The newcomer had found her way to the boat, drawn by the same pheromones that had attracted the first. Slowly, as if in a dream, Westwood turned round to look.

She had alighted on the deck. Her face was only inches from his. Her compound eyes sparkled like cut gems, black and shiny as onyx. Her armor shown gun-metal blue. Her wings shimmered, changing color in the moonlight, from orange to blue to silver. Her black antennae thumped and prodded Westwood, bashing him this way and that, as she examined him from head to toe. And then she sprang.

Westwood felt as if a ton of scrap metal had fallen on top of him. The back of his skull smacked loudly against the deck. His head swam from the blow. All around him was the screeching clamor of the she-wasp's armor, clanking, groaning, squealing and creaking as she tightened her grip upon him. Westwood knew what was coming. He tried to steel himself for the pain. But it was pointless. Nothing could prepare him for the blinding anguish of the she-wasp's embrace. When the stinger slid into his gut, he shrieked in agony. The pain was unearthly, beyond bearing. It seemed to go on forever. Then suddenly, it stopped. Westwood felt nothing at all. He could not move. He could not speak. But, strangely, he was not afraid. The poison had dulled his fear, as well as his pain. A strange tranquility suffused his body. As the wasp dug her claws into his flesh, he could hear and feel the ripping of muscle and skin. Yet it caused him no pain.

As if from far away, he heard the thunder of her wings. He knew she was lifting him from the deck. And suddenly they were airborne, soaring aloft. She carried him face down. He could see everything below. Westwood saw the boat in the muddy river, growing smaller and smaller as he rose into the air. He saw the crewmen firing their guns. He saw the searchlights rocking wildly across the trees. Tiny red tracer beams pierced the night.

And then the boat was gone. Westwood saw only shadows and moonlight. The wasp was flying high over the treetops. She was taking Westwood to her lair. Her claws dug deep into his sides and flanks. But Westwood felt nothing. No pain. No panic. Only a deep, dreamy languor. And there was something else, a strange new feeling quickening in his soul. It was awe and wonder. Perhaps even love. The wasp filled him with admiration, this she-demon of the night. Her power was overwhelming, intoxicating. And Westwood realized that he was grateful, yes, grateful, for the strength of her venom, which banished all pain and fear. "Maybe," he thought, hardly daring to hope, "maybe this isn't going to hurt after all."

ABOUT THE AUTHOR

Richard Poe is a *New York Times* bestselling author and an award-winning journalist. He has written widely on business, science, history and politics. Poe's books have sold nearly a million copies in the United States, and have been published in 21 foreign languages. Prior to *Perfect Fear*, Poe's last book was *The Shadow Party*, co-written with David Horowitz.

ACKNOWLEDGMENTS

First and foremost, I thank my wife Marie, who helped shape this book with sure and confident insight.

Very special thanks to Jennifer Basey Sander and Vanessa Perez, my former editor and art director respectively, from the good old days at Prima and Random House. Thanks also to Kelly and Rob, Masako and Dominik, Frank Martinez, and many others too numerous to name.

I offer a special prayer of thanks to St. Jude, help of the hopeless, and to the Blessed Mother, to whom this book is consecrated, under her titles of Our Lady of Fatima and Panagia ti Giatrissa, the Healing Virgin of Mani.